# Robbery at the Roller Derby

# Robbery at the Roller Derby

A Mollie McGhie Sailing Mystery

Prequel Novella

ELLEN JACOBSON

Robbery at the Roller Derby


Print ISBN: 978-1-951495-02-2
Digital ISBN: 978-1-951495-01-5
Large Print ISBN: 978-1-951495-03-9

Editor: Under Wraps Publishing
Cover Designer: Mariah Sinclair

First Printing: September 2019

Published by: Ellen Jacobson
www.ellenjacobsonauthor.com

For anyone who has ever wanted
a book dedicated to them.
Just fill in your name below and, presto,
you've got a book dedicated to you!

For ____________________________
(Your Name)

# CONTENTS

## CAST OF CHARACTERS

*Mollie (aka Darth Skater) Reynolds* – A member of the Wild Waitresses roller derby team, Mollie juggles skating practice with low-paying, mind-numbing temp jobs in corporate offices. She especially hates data-entry and spreadsheets.

*Scooter McGhie* – A nerdy telecommunications consultant who works in a corporate office. His idea of a fun Friday night is poring over spreadsheets and analyzing data.

*Carl Kowalski* – A lawyer who works in a—yes, you guessed it—a corporate office. He deals with spreadsheets and contracts on a daily basis.

*Kyle Jansen* – A security guard by day and a roller derby referee on the weekends. He has no idea what a spreadsheet is and doesn't really care either.

*Velma (aka Red Hot Mama) Manning* – A member of the Wild Waitresses' rival team, the Bruising Beauties, and a waitress at the Rock n' Roller diner. She wouldn't be caught dead using a spreadsheet.

*Henry Tyler* – A paramedic by profession, Henry volunteers as the Wild Waitresses' medic. He uses spreadsheets to inventory medical supplies and medication.

*Misty (aka Amazonia) Stephens* – A member of the Wild Waitresses, an elementary school teacher, and a cosmetology student. She's indifferent to spreadsheets.

*Leon LaBelle* – The Wild Waitresses' biggest fan and the founding member of the Wild Bunch. He attends every match even if he has to travel and keeps track of the team's stats in a spreadsheet.

*Eliza Dooley* – Manager of the Wild Waitresses, Eliza also owns the Rock n' Roller diner where she employs skaters as waitresses and the warehouse where they hold their matches. She uses spreadsheets to keep track of her business.

*The Gruesome Twosome* – Identical twins who skate on the Bruising Beauties roller derby team, as well as waitress part-time at the diner. They prefer their spreadsheets to look exactly the same.

# CHAPTER 1
# DARTH SKATER

As I waited for the referee to signal the start of the match, I wondered what my mother would think if she could see how I was dressed—a turquoise 1950s diner style waitress outfit with the number 51 on the back, purple and white striped knee socks over fishnet stockings, a helmet, knee-pads, and roller skates. She'd probably be stunned into silence for a few moments then proceed to tell me that turquoise doesn't really suit my fair complexion and mousy brown hair. After that, she'd look at my feet with despair.

"Mollie, roller skating is for kids, not for grown women who are almost thirty," she'd say with her hands on her hips. "It's about time you settled down and thought about your career instead of acting like a child. Besides, you know what a klutz you are. You're going to end up killing yourself on those things!"

The whistle blew, interrupting the maternal voice from adding to its long list of complaints about my lack of direction, the guys I dated, and not flossing my teeth on a regular basis. If she ever found out I was on a roller derby team, she'd definitely flip out. Although that might make her forget about my lack of steady employment and that my last boyfriend had been an accordion player in a punk rock band. She'd still harp on my neglected dental hygiene routine though. Some things never change.

Fortunately, I lived in Cleveland and her home base was far enough away that visits from her required the purchase of a plane ticket. It meant she was unlikely to discover that I was a member of the Wild Waitresses skating team as I'd be able to hide the evidence before she showed up.

Banishing thoughts of my mother from my head, I focused on my task at hand—zipping around the other skaters and taking the lead. I swiveled my hips and slid between two ferocious looking identical twins (they weren't called The Gruesome Twosome for nothing), then ducked under the outstretched arm of another opponent, narrowly avoiding decapitation.

After scooting past one more foe, I grinned and did a fist pump. Victory was in my sights. I only had a few more feet to go before crossing the line. A voice boomed out over the loudspeaker: "Darth Skater is out front! Look at her flying by!"

My smile was quickly wiped off my face as I felt a sharp jab on my side which sent me flying off the track and straight into the bleachers.

"Are you all right, miss?" a man's voice asked.

It took me a moment to realize where the sound was coming from. "How did I end up here?" I mumbled into the dark blue wool sweater that my face was currently pressed up against.

"You mean on my lap?" I lifted my head and saw a pair of dark brown puppy dog eyes looking at me with concern. "That was quite a nasty fall you took. You should probably get checked out and make sure you don't have a concussion."

I rubbed my temples. "Nah, I feel okay," I said before glancing down at the red marks on my legs. "Other than a little fishnet burn and another pair of ruined stockings, I'm still good to go. I just need a band-aid or two to stop the bleeding and—"

"Blood?" he interrupted, his voice trembling.

I examined my right arm. "Just a little."

The person sitting next to us chuckled. "Be careful, you're going to make him faint. He can't stand the sight of blood."

I glanced over and saw a stocky man with a blond goatee smiling at me. "Hey, I know you," I said. "You're Misty's boyfriend. Carl, right?"

"That's me," he said. "Let me introduce you to the man whose lap you're sitting on. This is Scooter.

Scooter, this is Mollie, or Darth Skater as she's known when in skates. It's my pal's first time at a roller derby match. I don't think he expected this much excitement ... or blood, though."

Scooter looked like he was going to be ill.

"Are you going to be okay?" I asked, noting the blood draining from his face. "Maybe you're the one who should see the medic."

He took a deep breath. "I'll be fine."

"That didn't sound very convincing. You don't look fine to me. Are you normally this pale?"

He smiled. "Shouldn't you be out there skating or something?"

"I should be. I've got a match to win." As I scooted off his lap, I heard a crunching sound. I looked down and saw a pair of tortoiseshell glasses underneath one of my roller skates.

"I was wondering where those went," Scooter said.

"They must have gone flying when Mollie landed in your lap," Carl said.

I handed the mangled glasses to Scooter. The lenses were still intact, but one of the arms had broken off the frames completely. My shoulders slumped. "Sorry. I'll get them fixed for you."

He shook his head. "Don't worry about it."

Before I could argue with him, someone tapped me on my shoulder. I turned and saw Kyle, the head referee, scowling at me. "If you're done flirting, would you mind joining the rest of us back on the track?"

"Flirting?" I raised my eyebrows. "Does it look like I'm flirting?"

Kyle snorted. "You were sitting on some guy's lap. Do you have another explanation?"

I looked over at Scooter. He had color back in his face, but I couldn't tell if he was bright red from being embarrassed or because he was angry at Kyle for giving me a hard time.

"The reason I'm over here is because of Velma," I said, pointing at the skater who had slammed into me. She made an obscene gesture before pulling her long russet-colored hair into a ponytail. It was no surprise that her skater name was Red Hot Mama—not only was she a redhead, she also had a red-hot temper, which she took out on the rest of us especially on the track.

"Penalty for arguing with the referee," Kyle said.

"You've got to be kidding me," I snapped. "Velma elbowed me, then tripped me. She's the one who should be penalized. And she just gave me the finger!"

"You just earned yourself another penalty. Want to go for three?"

I inched forward on my roller skates and jabbed my finger in Kyle's chest. "I don't think you're smart enough to count to three."

He grabbed my hand and twisted it before pushing me back.

"Hey, that's enough," Scooter said rising to his feet. "Can't you see that she's injured?"

Carl pointed at the floor. "Yeah, there's blood dripping everywhere."

"Fine. Go get yourself checked out," Kyle said. Then he leaned forward and whispered in my ear. "Better watch yourself. Roller derby can be a dangerous sport. You've been causing enough trouble for me lately. I'd hate to see you get hurt."

***

"Stop squirming," Henry, our team medic, said. He applied antibiotic cream to the cut on my arm. "It doesn't look too bad. Not like last month when you banged your head against the railing. Now that was a nasty spill. Thank goodness you had been wearing a helmet. Otherwise, you would have needed far more than stitches."

I pointed at my left eyebrow. "Can you still see the scar?"

Henry squinted. "Hard to see anything underneath all that purple glitter."

"You can blame Misty for the eye shadow. Ever since she's been taking that cosmetology course, she's been using me as her guinea pig. Apparently, glitter and false eyelashes are all the rage."

"If you say so." Henry chuckled. "Fortunately, my daughter is too young to wear make-up." He reached into his medical kit grabbing a gauze pad and surgical tape. "Hold your arm steady."

"Don't you have anything more colorful?" I asked as he dressed my wound. "White is so boring."

"It's a bandage, not a fashion accessory."

"No reason why medical supplies can't be fashionable."

He finished applying the dressing, then said, "I think I have something for you." He rummaged in the kit, pushing aside other boring medical supplies, including some scalpels, a splint, and a cold pack, before pulling out a bright green band-aid. "Will this do?"

"Are those little cats on there?" I asked.

"Yep. I also have some with dinosaurs. They're part of the stash I have on hand for kids." He grinned. "And adults who haven't quite grown up yet. You have a small scratch on your other arm. Why don't we stick it there?"

"I love it," I said after he pressed it on.

"I thought you might." Henry handed me another band-aid. "Here's an extra one. Goodness knows you'll probably end up needing it."

As I tucked the band-aid in the pocket of my waitress outfit, one of the referees blew his whistle, signaling half-time. Misty skated over and plopped down on the bench next to me, stretching her long legs out in front of her. She was six feet tall barefoot and at least six feet four inches when she had her skates on. It was no wonder her skater name was

Amazonia. She towered over everyone else on the track.

"Did the doc get you all fixed up?" she asked.

"I'm not a doctor." Henry frowned. "I didn't have enough money for med school, so I had to settle for being a paramedic."

"Hey, paramedics are important," Misty said, patting his arm. "You guys are the first at the scene and save lives. Don't diminish what you do."

"Don't get me wrong," he said. "I love what I do. It's a real adrenaline rush being an ambulance driver and dealing with emergencies." He shrugged his shoulders. "But sometimes, I wish they paid me the kind of money that doctors make. Money's tight sometimes, especially raising two kids on my own. I have to work side gigs to be able to afford childcare and put food on the table."

"I hear you," I said. "I can barely make ends meet and that's without children. Maybe my mom's right and I need to start looking for a real job instead of working as a temp."

"Sounds like a topic to talk about over drinks tonight." Misty pointed at the track. "But before that, we need to get you back out there. The Bruising Beauties are crushing us. Velma scored four points while you've been sitting on the sidelines."

"She probably did it by cheating." I turned to Henry. "You have a good view of the track from here. You must have seen how she elbowed me. It was vicious. And then Kyle penalized me and not her. Maybe you could go talk to that jerk and tell him what really happened."

Henry held up his hands. "I'm just here to provide first-aid, not to get involved in disputes over the match. Besides, Kyle isn't exactly a guy I want to mess with, nor should you for that matter."

"Why's that?" I asked.

"Forget I said anything." He pushed his shaggy brown hair out of his eyes, then busied himself stowing his supplies back into his kit.

"Come on, it's just us," I said. "We can keep a secret."

The medic laughed. "Misty might be able to keep a secret, but you, not so much."

"Are you ever going to let that go?" I said. "It was an honest mistake."

"What happened?" Misty asked.

"A couple of years ago, I planned this whole surprise party for my ex-wife. Mollie was supposed to pick up the birthday cake and what did she do? She brought my ex with her to the bakery."

"I can't help it if she asked me for a ride. And how was I supposed to know she'd open the box and see her name on it?" I put my head in my hands for a moment, then peeked up at Henry. "I'm really sorry it happened."

"It's okay," Henry said. "Our marriage was already on the rocks. A surprise party wasn't going to fix anything." He stood and pulled both of us to our feet. "That's enough about me. You girls better get back out there. You've got to stage a comeback in the second half." He wagged his finger at me. "And I better not see you back over here begging for more band-aids."

As Misty and I skated back toward our teammates, I asked her what the real story was between Henry and Kyle.

"It's actually all about the ex-wife," she said as she adjusted the strap on her helmet. "Kyle's the reason why she left Henry. They had been having an affair."

"I didn't know that," I said.

"It isn't exactly something that Henry talks about. She ended up dumping Kyle not long after that. And then you know the rest of the story. She hooked up with another guy, moved out to California and left those poor kids behind."

"Just goes to show you that you can't trust someone who opens up a cake box, sees their name on it, and complains that it has chocolate frosting instead of vanilla. He's better off without her. And it sounds like Kyle got what he deserved."

* * *

"Can you believe the nerve of that guy?" I asked Misty as we headed toward the locker room at the end of the match. "We could have won if Kyle hadn't singled me out again and gave me another penalty!"

I clenched my hands as I thought about how the Gruesome Twosome had joined forces with Velma and spread out across the track like a wall in an effort to keep me from passing them. I had feinted to the left, then quickly changed direction to pass on their right. Velma spun around to face me, got one of her skates tangled up between my feet and stumbled, bringing the twins down with her.

Kyle sided with Velma when she claimed that I had deliberately tripped her. The Wild Waitresses ended up losing the match after having to play short-handed while I fumed on the sidelines.

"It was a pretty bold move on Velma's part," my friend said as she tucked her helmet under her arm. "I couldn't believe it when she—"

She was interrupted by a middle-aged man with piercing blue eyes sitting in a wheelchair. He was parked directly in front of the hallway leading to the locker room. It was his favorite spot as it offered a good vantage point of the track, as well as given him the opportunity to intercept members of the Wild Waitresses. "Can I get your autograph?" he asked Misty.

"Sure, Leon." She smiled as he passed her a marker. "But don't you already have enough items with my signature? Wasn't it a t-shirt last week and a baseball hat the week before that? The other ladies on the team would be happy to sign autographs for you too. Like Mollie here."

Leon stared at me for a moment before he shook his head, and then handed Misty a poster of the team. "Can you sign here?" he asked, pointing at a spot underneath her picture. He watched intently as she inscribed her name. "Can you add, 'For your number one fan'?"

"No problem," she said sweetly.

Leon carefully rolled up his poster and tucked it in his backpack. I noticed that he had a whole selection of souvenirs with the Wild Waitresses logo on it including a water bottle, a turquoise scarf, a sweatshirt, a key chain with a miniature roller skate attached to it, and one of those giant foam fingers. "Thanks," he said. "I'll see you at the exhibition match next weekend."

"You realize it's an away game in Columbus," I said. "Are you really going to travel all that way just to see us play?"

"Of course," he said seriously. "I haven't missed a single game since the Wild Waitresses formed three years ago."

"You really are our number one fan," Misty said as she waved goodbye.

As I pushed the door to the locker room open, I looked back and saw Leon watching us. I shuddered and steered Misty inside. "He's a little creepy, don't you think?"

"Leon? No. He's harmless. If it wasn't for folks like

him, we wouldn't be able to do this. How do you think we pay for the track, equipment, and all the other costs that go into our matches? We need fans who buy tickets and show up every week."

"Well, there are fans and then there are stalkers."

"He's not a stalker," Misty said as she sat down on a bench and untied her skates. "You're too suspicious of people. Sure, he might be a little overenthusiastic, but it's not like he's an ax murderer or anything."

I rolled my eyes. "It's not like murderers wear badges that say 'Hello!' with their name written underneath, followed by 'I can't be trusted with an ax.' You don't even know if they're around until a dead body turns up. I'm telling you, it always turns out to be the last person you suspected, like an autograph-seeking roller derby fanatic."

"Instead of Darth Skater, maybe your skater name should be something Nancy Drew-related, like Nancy Drew Blood. You've always got your nose in those mystery books. Heaven help the police if you ever discover a dead body and decide to investigate."

"Like that will ever happen. I try to stay as far away from the police as I can. They're such sticklers for rules and regulations."

"See, that's what surprises me. You always say that you don't like to follow rules, but you would never cheat when it comes to roller derby, not like Velma does. You even go out of your way to make sure everyone knows when she breaks the rules."

I grinned. "That's different. Some rules are meant to be followed, others, well ... they're just stupid."

Misty ran her fingers through her long blond hair. "I'm going to have to do something with this before dinner. I've got helmet head." She gave me an appraising look. "We should run a straightener through your hair too. Get rid of that frizz. I also need to touch up your make-up."

"Why? All I'm planning on doing is heading home, crawling into bed with a box of Oreo cookies, and watching old movies. I'm exhausted and I'm starting a new temp job tomorrow. I really need a decent night's sleep."

"Did you forget about our double date tonight?"

I rubbed my temples. "Is that tonight?"

"Yep. I think you're going to like this fellow. He's a friend of Carl's."

"How many times are you going to fix me up on blind dates before you realize that I'm not really blind date material. The guys always smile and make polite conversation, but I never hear from them again."

Misty stuffed her socks in her skates and pushed herself off the bench. As she strode toward the lockers on the other side of the room, she said over her shoulder, "That's because you always start talking about ..."

"Talking about what?" I asked while removing my knee-pads. When she didn't respond, I called out, "Earth to Misty."

"My locker," she said in a shaky voice. "Someone broke into my locker."

I walked over to where she was standing. The metal door was ajar, and the contents of the locker were strewn onto the floor. I knelt and picked up a padlock that was nestled on top of Misty's down coat. "It looks like someone cut this with bolt cutters."

Misty took the padlock from my hand and inspected it. "How do you know it was bolt cutters?"

"Because that's what you use when you want to get into something that's padlocked." I handed her the items on the floor one-by-one and she placed them on a nearby table. "Is anything missing?"

"I'm not sure. Let me look." She chewed on her lip while she surveyed her possessions—a toiletry bag, a pink wool hat with matching mittens, high-heeled boots, sneakers, a small duffel bag, and a garment bag. She opened the garment bag first and pulled out a pair of dress pants and a silk blouse, presumably for her date with Carl. As she tucked the outfit back in the bag, something fluttered off the table. "I think this is yours," she said as she handed me the colorful band-aid Henry had given me earlier.

"Thanks, it must have fallen out of my pocket."

Next she rummaged through the duffel bag which contained the clothes she had worn to the track earlier that day. Finally, she looked through her toiletry bag, which contained an insane number of glitter eye shadow palettes, along with several brushes, styling tools, and hair accessories.

"Well?" I prompted. "Is everything there?"

She hesitated for a moment. "Did you see my purse anywhere?"

I peered into the locker. "Here it is," I said. "It was at the back."

After checking her wallet, she paused for a moment, then said, "It looks like the only thing that's missing is my scarf."

"That's a relief," I said. "But a bit weird. Who would break open a locker just to steal a scarf?"

Her knuckles turned white as she gripped the sides of the table. "I don't know."

"Well, there's only one way to find out. Start asking questions." I pointed at the women huddled by the showers rehashing the match. We shared the locker room and the arena with the Bruising Beauties, so there was a lot of boasting going on about which team had the better moves. "Hey, ladies, can I have your attention," I said, waving my hand in the air. "Misty's—"

Misty pulled my arm down. "Can we keep this between us," she said in an undertone.

"What happened?" one of the Gruesome Twosome twins asked.

"It's nothing," Misty said. "Just a little misunderstanding. Go back to what you were doing."

"Why are we keeping this a secret?" I whispered.

Misty gripped my hand tightly. "We just are, okay?

Promise me, you won't say anything to anyone." She grabbed her purse. "I've got to take care of something. Why don't I meet you and the guys at the Rock n' Roller diner at seven?"

"Hey, wait a minute," I called out. "You don't have any shoes on."

When she didn't respond, I knew something was seriously wrong. Misty had this weird phobia about her toes and wouldn't be caught dead running around in public barefoot if she could help it. I found it hard to believe that she was so upset about a missing scarf that she'd show the world her toes, even if they did have glitter nail polish on them.

# CHAPTER 2
# NINJA UNICORNS

After Misty left, I tucked her belongings back into her locker and closed the door. Although her padlock didn't work anymore, I figured her stuff was safer inside the locker rather than strewn out on the table. The last thing she needed was for something else to go missing while she was off on her mysterious errand.

Next, I changed out of my team uniform and into my street clothes. After pulling on my favorite pair of cowboy boots, I stood in front of the full-length mirror by the showers. Remembering Misty's dressy outfit, I sighed as I stared at my old tattered jeans and sweatshirt. Sure, the unicorn ninjas on my top were cute—I loved how their sparkly horns peeked out from their hoods—but I wasn't sure it was the best look for a blind date, especially coupled with the purple glitter eye shadow which had somehow migrated from my eyelids down on to my cheeks.

It was going to take industrial strength makeup remover to get that goop off my face. Fortunately, I had a giant jar of the stuff back at home, a gift that my mother had given me during her last visit, along with a year's supply of dental floss. I checked my watch. I had just enough time to get back to my apartment, take a quick shower, apply understated makeup, and find something more suitable to wear before I had to meet Misty, Carl, and my blind date.

As I shrugged on my coat, a stylishly dressed older woman came over. "Do you want to pick up a shift tonight? Velma went home sick during the match and I'm short-handed." Eliza was the driving force behind the Wild Waitresses. Not only did she manage our team, she also had bought the old warehouse we played in and overseen the set-up of a flat roller derby track, bleachers, and other facilities in the cavernous space. She was in the process of renovating the building, creating further usable space including offices which she leased out. And, if that wasn't enough, she owns the Rock n' Roller diner, a local attraction and a popular hangout for the skating community.

"I really wish I could, but I have a date tonight." Eliza knew that I was often short of cash and offered me shifts when she could. I groaned at the thought of the money I'd be missing out on. Patrons of the diner were usually generous tippers. They loved the kitschy feel of the place from the roller-skating waitresses spinning around the joint to the 1950s diner feel complete with red vinyl booths, black and white tiled floor, and a jukebox.

"Who's the date with?"

"No idea. Some guy Misty's new boyfriend knows," I said. "We're meeting at the diner. If it doesn't go well, maybe I can ditch him and waitress instead."

"I'm sure it will be fine. If not, at least you'll get a good meal out of it. We have chocolate fudge brownie sundaes on the menu tonight for dessert."

"Well, if that isn't a reason to stick it out to the end of a date, I don't know what is."

"I'll make sure to set one aside for you." Her eyes twinkled. "I know how much you love chocolate."

"That's why I took up skating," I said. "Given the amount of chocolate I go through each week, I need some sort of exercise to burn all those calories off."

"Most girls just go to the gym. They don't usually sign up for a roller derby team."

"Gyms have never been my thing. Everyone is so serious there. Then, when I heard about the Wild Waitresses and saw the outfits you guys wear—I mean come on, fishnet stockings and knee socks, how cool is that—I was hooked. If you're going to sweat, you might as well have fun doing it."

Eliza patted me on the back. "Well, you're a great

addition to the team. It's a shame you keep getting all those penalties though."

"Talk to Kyle," I said. "He's got it in for me. None of the other refs hand out penalties like he does."

"He does seem to be on edge lately." She frowned. "I know he's been going through a rough patch. He got laid off, you know."

"He worked down at the auto plant, right?" Eliza nodded. "I suppose being out of work might explain why he's always in a bad mood. But I seem to be the target of his cranky temperament."

Eliza pursed her lips. "Maybe you should cut him some slack."

"I'll think about it." I thought back to earlier in the match when I had landed on Scooter's lap and Kyle had given me a hard time. At the time, when he'd said that roller derby was a dangerous sport and hoped I didn't get hurt, it had seemed like a threat. Perhaps I had misinterpreted things. Maybe his anxiousness over being unemployed made him lash out.

Anxiety can make you do crazy things and I should know. Ask me about the time that I went to a sci-fi convention dressed as Chewbacca and entered a karaoke contest. Actually, you know what, let's pretend I didn't mention that. Some things are better left forgotten.

"So, what do you say?" Eliza asked, interrupting my thoughts about Star Wars costumes you really shouldn't wear especially if you're short.

"Say about what?"

"About asking Kyle to join the team for drinks after practice on Wednesday. It might help cheer him up."

"Why not," I said, vowing to try to be more understanding of the referee. "We should ask Henry too. He seems like he's under a lot of pressure as well, with his job and family life. I bet he could use a break."

"Yeah, why not? We'll make a little party of it. I'll let everyone know. Now, you better go get ready for your date." She cocked her head to one side. "You were planning to do something about that makeup, weren't you?"

* * *

I left the arena through the back entrance where the bus stop was located. It was close to dusk, and I had to shield my eyes from the glare of the setting sun. Shivering from the unseasonably cold air blowing in off of Lake Erie, I tucked my scarf around my neck and pulled on my gloves. One of these days, I was going to have to move some place warmer, like Florida.

Visions of sipping tropical drinks while lounging on a beach and reading a good book filled my head. As I neared the side of the building, a wind gust blew my hat off my head, bringing me sharply back to the reality of spending yet another cold winter in Ohio. As I bent to pick it up, I heard a woman pleading with someone.

"I'm telling you, I don't have it," she said. "Please, you have to believe me."

A man's voice replied gruffly, "Why should I believe you? You have it in for me, just like everyone else."

"You're being paranoid," she replied. "No one has it in for you."

"Then where did it go? Obviously, it didn't walk away by itself, now did it? That means you have it. You stole it from me!"

"Please, don't. I'm telling you the truth," the woman said in a shaky voice that sounded very familiar. I hurried around the corner and saw Misty, pressed against the brick wall. Kyle was standing in front of her brandishing something metallic in his hand.

"Get away from her!" I shouted.

The referee turned his head and glared at me before taking a few steps back. "What are you doing here?" he asked as he shoved his hands in his jacket pockets. "This doesn't concern you."

"Of course, it does," I said, trying to sound more confident than I felt. "You're threatening my friend."

"Threatening. You're nuts." Kyle scoffed. "Misty and I are just shooting the breeze."

"It doesn't look like that from where I'm standing."

I turned to Misty. "Are you okay?"

As Misty took a few cautious steps toward me, she said, "I'm fine. Really, it's nothing."

"He was holding a knife on you," I said.

She furrowed her brow. "A knife?"

"I saw it. He had something metallic in his hand."

Kyle gave a brittle laugh. "You mean this?" He pulled a small silver digital camera out of his pocket. "I was showing Misty some pictures."

"No, there was a knife. I swear." I reached forward and patted his jacket.

"Find what you're looking for?" he asked, holding his arms out at his side, the camera dangling from a cord in his hand.

I felt a small object in his left pocket, just the right size to be a pocketknife. "Aha!" I said as I yanked it out. Then the huge grin plastered across my face faded as I realized what I was holding.

"I didn't know you smoked," Kyle said sarcastically. He plucked the cigarette lighter from my hand before putting his arm around Misty's shoulders. "Take care of what we talked about or else."

She gulped. "I don't—"

Kyle held up his hand, cutting her off mid-sentence. "Just do what I said."

As he stormed off toward the parking lot, I grabbed Misty's hand and squeezed it. "What the heck is going on?"

She pulled her hand away and wrapped her arms around herself. "It's nothing."

"It's not nothing, that's for sure." Misty was trembling, probably due in part to the fact that she was outside barefoot and still in her skating uniform. Still I also had a feeling her conversation with Kyle had a something to do with it.

"We're not done talking about this," I said. "But first we need to get you warmed up."

After accompanying Misty back into the locker room where she changed clothes, she finally broke down and told me what was going on.

"Before the match, Kyle asked me to store something in my locker," she said, wringing her hands in her lap. "It wasn't there when we checked my stuff."

"I thought you said it was a scarf that had been taken."

"True. My scarf is missing." She chewed on her bottom lip. "Or maybe I left it at home. I'm not sure."

"What exactly did Kyle give you and why couldn't he hang onto it himself?"

"He said it was some ... um ... jewelry that had belonged to his mom. He was going to take it to the pawnshop after the game for some extra cash. He didn't want to leave it in his bag out in the open inside the arena. He was worried it would get stolen."

I shook my head. "Why in the world did you agree to take care of something so valuable?"

"I don't know. He's been hard up lately." She ran her fingers through her hair. "I thought I could help and now look what's happened."

"It's not your fault," I said. "Besides, his reaction was way out of line. You were doing him a favor. He can't hold you responsible."

"But he does and if I don't find it, he's going to ..." Her voice trailed off as she stared blankly at the floor.

"He's going to do what?" I asked softly.

"Nothing. He just needs it back so he can get the money and pay his rent."

"Sounds like his problem, not yours. Tell him to call the police and they can investigate."

Misty blinked rapidly. "Trust me, calling the police isn't a good idea."

I narrowed my eyes. "There's more going on here then you're telling me."

"There is, but I can't talk about it. At least not now. I need to find the missing package and I need your help doing it."

"Me?"

"Remember how we were talking about those mysteries you read? You're always bragging about how you can figure out whodunit before the end of the book."

"You do realize fiction isn't the same thing as real life, right?"

"Come on. It'll be fun. You always wanted to be a detective," she said, straightening her back. "Now, we better hurry up and get ready for our double date." She pulled out a compact from her toiletry bag. "What do you think of green eye shadow?"

# CHAPTER 3
# ALIEN INVASION

"Are you sure you want to do this?" I asked Misty as we walked through the entrance to the Rock n' Roller diner. "After what you've been through with the robbery and Kyle, I'm sure Carl would understand if you canceled the date."

She paused by the hostess station and pressed her lips together. "Promise me you won't tell Carl what happened."

"Why don't you want him to know? He's your boyfriend. He'll want to help."

"Of course, he'll want to help. He likes to fix things, and he's great at fixing things like broken bookshelves, but this is different. If he finds out what happened, he'll tell me to call the police. Or he'll do it himself." She smiled. "He's the complete opposite of you when it comes to following the rules, always on the straight and narrow. You know his brother and father are cops, right? He was under a lot of pressure to join the force, but he became a lawyer instead and a corporate one at that. His family feels like he sold his soul for money."

"That's how I feel sometimes working in cubicles at corporate offices, except when you're a temp instead of a high-powered attorney, your soul is worth quite a lot less money."

"Try being an elementary school teacher. We hardly make anything and whatever extra I do have left over each month goes into buying supplies for my classroom."

"Yeah, but at least you're doing something noble. I'm not sure what value mind-numbing data entry truly adds to the world."

One of the Gruesome Twosome twins skated up to us holding a tray fully laden with hot fudge brownie sundaes. "Your dates are at a table by the window," she said before spinning around and depositing the desserts at one of the booths lining the wall. I was always surprised that Eliza hired members of our rival team to waitress at her diner given how competitive she was when it came to roller derby. Still even I had to admit that the Bruising Beauties were nice ladies when off the track. Well, that is, everyone except Velma.

As we walked toward the back of the restaurant, Misty made me pinky swear not to tell Carl about what had happened. I agreed provided she promised not to tell my blind date about that whole Chewbacca karaoke debacle.

"There she is. Gorgeous as always," Carl said as he embraced Misty.

She did look gorgeous with her perfectly styled hair and date-worthy outfit. I, on the other hand, hadn't had time to go home and change. I was still sporting my ninja unicorn sweatshirt and old jeans, but at least my glitter eye shadow had been removed and replaced with a neutral brown tone.

Carl turned to me. "I think you already know your date. But don't worry. You don't have to sit on his lap this time. There's plenty of room for you to have your own seat." I felt my face grow warm as I gazed into Scooter's dark brown eyes once again, his broken glasses perched on his nose.

Misty broke out laughing. "Surprise! See it's not a blind date after all. You two already know each other."

As Scooter stood to pull out my chair for me, I noticed his face was nearly as red as mine felt. After he sat down across from me, I asked him to hand me his glasses and the broken-off arm. I tried to ignore the shiver that went down my spine as his fingers brushed against mine. Starting off a blind date feeling a twinge of attraction was a bad omen, at least based on my relationship history with the now long gone accordion player.

"Let me see what I can do about fixing these temporarily." I pulled a roll of duct tape out of my purse, tore off a few pieces, and reattached the arm. "Try them on."

"Better than new," Scooter said as he positioned them behind his ears. "Do you always carry duct tape with you?"

"Yep. You never know when it's going to come in handy."

"She pulled a pair of pliers out of there just last week," Misty said.

"Pliers?" Scooter asked.

"I needed to get something open," I said.

Scooter eyed my purse. "Good thing you were able to do it with pliers. I don't think anything larger—like bolt cutters—would fit in there."

"Bolt cutters." I gave Scooter an appraising look. What were the chances that he would mention exactly what had been used to break open Misty's locker? I really hoped he wasn't a mind reader, because I sure didn't want him to know that his smile was making me weak in the knees. "That's an interesting tool to bring up."

"I thought it would sound more impressive than a screwdriver."

"You're right. Screwdrivers are pretty boring." I tapped my lips with my finger. "Except for maybe hammers. They top the list of least exciting tools."

"I bet you'd be a lot of fun at the hardware store,"

Scooter said, his eyes twinkling. "Maybe we could go there for our next date. Check out the latest line of bolt cutters."

Misty kicked me under the table. "Enough talk about tools. Let's order."

While we looked at the menus, I glanced at Scooter. He had already mentioned a second date, he had a good sense of humor, and he didn't seem embarrassed to be wearing glasses covered in duct tape out in public. Maybe this guy was different. If this worked out, I'd have to reevaluate my whole stance on blind dates. Who knows, maybe I'd even start fixing people up myself.

* * *

Over cheeseburgers and fries, we tried to explain roller derby to Scooter. I'm not sure what he found more confusing—our skater names or the concept of a jammer.

"Think of it like this," Carl suggested. "The jammer —"

"That's me," I interjected. "You can tell when I'm the jammer, because I have a star on my helmet."

"So, the jammer races around the track," Carl continued, "trying to pass as many members of the other team as possible."

"You get one point for each person you pass," I said. "And the blockers from the other team do their best to keep you from getting by."

"That's it?" Scooter asked before snagging a fry off of my plate. When I pulled my plate back, he smiled sheepishly. "Sorry, I thought you were done."

Misty drummed her fingers on the table. "What did you mean by 'That's it'?"

"Well to be honest, there isn't a ball involved. I'm used to sports where you have to dunk a ball, or kick a ball into a goal, or run with a ball across an end line, or even putt a ball into a hole."

Carl whistled. "Man, didn't you see what these chicks do out there on the track? It's deadly. And they do it on skates. I'd rather take my chances with dribbling a ball across a court any day of the week."

Scooter held up his hands. "Point taken. I saw what happened to Mollie. Or should I say, Darth Skater. That's a play on Darth Vader, right? I take it you're a Star Trek fan."

My jaw dropped. Maybe this blind date was going downhill after all. Who mixes up Star Trek and Star Wars?

Misty took one look at my face and broke out in peals of laughter. "Even I know that Darth Vader is from Star Wars, not Star Trek."

"Well, now I've stuck my foot in it," Scooter said.

"Isn't there a Star Wars movie marathon in a couple of weeks?" Misty asked. "Maybe you could take him along with you for educational purposes."

Scooter's eyes lit up. "That sounds fun. We can

even stop by the hardware store afterward."

"Really?" I asked. "You would sit through all those movies back-to-back?"

"They serve popcorn, don't they?" He didn't miss a beat and I nodded. "Then, I'm in."

"Well, I'd say this calls for dessert," Misty said. "Another match-making success on my part."

* * *

"So, why did you hurry me away from the table to the ladies' room?" I asked Misty. "I barely got to finish the last bite of my sundae."

My friend finished touching up her eyeliner, then applied more lipstick. "I think you were starting to scare Scooter off."

"All I did was ask whether he had ever seen a UFO."

"Exactly my point."

"But he agreed to go see Star Wars. He has to be open to the possibility."

"There's a big difference between believing in UFOs, alien abductions, and going to see a movie. Besides, he agreed to go because of you," she said as she sprayed some perfume on her wrists. "He thinks you're cute."

"He does?"

"He does," she said firmly. "And he's a nice guy with a good job. Even your mother would approve."

"I doubt it. She'd find something about him that didn't live up to her exacting standards." I tried to smooth down my frizzy hair with a damp brush. "Did you see his smile? He has nice teeth too. I bet he flosses regularly. That might be a point in his favor with my mom."

Misty grabbed the brush from my hand. "You're only making it worse. Let me." When she was done, my locks looked sleek and glossy. She pulled out one of her glitter eye shadows. "You sure you don't want to liven your eyes up?"

"Ah, no. I think I'll leave the glitter for the track. We should probably get back to the table, anyway."

As we exited the ladies' room, Leon waved to us. He was at a table with three other guys, all of them dressed in Wild Waitresses sweatshirts and hats. They called themselves the Wild Bunch and met up at the Rock n' Roller after each game to analyze the team's performance.

"Come look at this new spreadsheet I set up," Leon said. "I enter the stats from each match and it generates these nifty charts."

"That is cool," Misty said. "Come have a look, Mollie."

"No thanks. I get enough of spreadsheets at work."

Misty nudged me. "But your spreadsheets don't have the team logo at the top. See that roller skate with the laces spelling out two Ws for the Wild Waitresses?"

I leaned forward to get a better view of his laptop screen. "That is pretty cool," I said grudgingly. "So, is that what you do at each match—take note of everything that happens?"

"Yep. Me and the rest of the Wild Bunch. We all sit at different vantage points in the arena so that between us we see all the action."

"And your spot is right in front of the locker room," I said.

He nodded while moving his cursor on the screen and clicking open another file. "I'm positioned there at least thirty minutes before the first whistle and I don't budge either until the match is over."

"You don't ever take a break? Say to go get a soft pretzel or maybe a can of pop?"

"Nope. The other guys would never forgive me if I missed anything. Besides, it would skew our stats."

I considered this for a few moments. The way Leon positioned himself meant that anyone entering or exiting the locker room had to pass right by him through a narrow gap between his wheelchair and the hallway wall. Our team had gone into the locker room toward the end of halftime for a pep talk from Eliza. Misty and I had been the last ones to leave as she had insisted on touching up my eye shadow. I remembered her tucking the toiletry bag back inside her locker before securing the door with the padlock. Meaning that whoever had broken into her locker had done so during the second half of the match. When I asked Leon if anyone had passed by him after halftime, he scratched his chin before answering.

"Let's see. Henry Tyler came by right after Misty whipped you around the Gruesome Twosome. Now that was an awesome sight."

"Henry the medic?" I asked. "What was he doing going into the locker room? He wouldn't have any reason to be there. If he needed the men's room, there are public restrooms on the other side of the arena."

"I didn't ask him. I had more important stuff to be doing," he said, tapping on his computer. "He was in there for about ten minutes."

"Okay, did anyone else go into the locker room?"

"Toward the end of the match, Velma came running past me. She looked like she was going to be ill." It jibed with what Eliza had said about the Red Hot Mama not feeling so hot and missing her shift at the diner. "She came back out about twenty minutes later. I asked her for her autograph, but she ignored me."

"Wait a minute," Misty said. "You get autographs from the Bruising Beauties?"

Leon shrugged his shoulders. "Sure. Why not? Velma is one of the top skaters in the country. You never know, one day her signature might be worth a lot of money."

Misty sniffed. "Did you think he only stalked you?" I whispered to her.

"What was that?" Leon asked.

"I was just wondering if you saw anyone else," I said.

"You mean other than Eliza?"

"Eliza went into the locker room?" I asked. "I can't believe she would leave the track during our match."

"I think she went in to check on Velma," Leon said.

I frowned. "Wait, that doesn't make sense. Velma isn't even on our team. Why would she be checking on her?"

"You sure do have a lot of questions," Leon said. "What's this about, anyway?"

Before I could reply, Misty grabbed my elbow. "We really should get back to our dates. Thanks again for showing us your spreadsheets. It's really impressive." As we walked away, she added, "I think Nancy Drew wasn't so obvious when she was asking questions."

"Okay, so maybe I'm no Nancy Drew, but we got some critical information, right?" I paused and counted on my fingers. "We have three suspects—Henry, Velma, and Eliza. Now all we have to do is—"

A loud crashing noise interrupted me. One of the Gruesome Twosome came sliding across the floor, coming to a halt at our feet, her tray clattering behind her. She clutched her right arm. "I think it's broken," she said before turning her head to look at the other side of the diner. I followed her gaze. There, standing at the hostess station was Velma, looking fit as a fiddle. "It's her fault," the injured woman said before letting out a loud groan.

# CHAPTER 4
# MIND-NUMBING DATA ENTRY

The next day, I had a tussle with my alarm clock, then dragged myself out of bed and into the kitchen. I always need at least two mochas before I can function in the morning. Unfortunately, I have a hard time operating small appliances until I've had my caffeine fix which makes it extremely difficult. I need coffee to operate the machine that makes coffee, but I can't get coffee until I operate the machine. I could only hope that one of these days my lottery numbers would pay off and then I could hire someone to bring me coffee in bed. Today was definitely not that day. So, I fired up the espresso machine and waited for the chaos to ensue. And boy, did it ever ensue.

When I tried to open a new bag of ground coffee, the bag exploded covering my new Princess Leia pajamas in a thick coating of dark brown powder. Next, I scalded my hand while steaming milk. After running cold water over the burn, I stirred a spoonful of chocolate syrup into the milk and poured it into a mug. Okay, confession time, it wasn't just one spoonful. More like half the syrup container. With my new temp job starting this morning, I was going to need plenty of chocolate to make it through a long day of sitting in a cubicle and staring at a computer.

Finally, I went to grab the espresso from the machine to add to my warm chocolate milk, only to find it dribbling off the counter and onto the floor. Yep somehow, I had forgotten to place a cup underneath the nozzle for the espresso to drip into. Nothing like a little chaos to start your Monday morning off right.

By this point, I was running late for work. I had just enough time to change into a black pencil skirt and dark gray turtleneck sweater, run the straightener through my hair, and toss my pajamas in the laundry basket. The mess in the kitchen would have to wait until I got back.

I boarded the bus and tried to mask my jealousy of the folks sipping their steaming cups of coffee. I'm not sure I did a very good job with the whole hiding-my-envy thing, because the lady I was sitting next to looked like she was afraid I was going to steal her Americano. Just for the record, I didn't, although I was sorely tempted.

After a thirty minute ride, I disembarked near the Terminal Tower and trudged into one of the nearby office buildings. The smell of roasted coffee beans wafted from a kiosk in the lobby. I glanced at my watch, then scowled at the long line of people waiting to order. There was no way I was going to have time to grab a coffee before I was due upstairs.

As I pressed the elevator button, I heard someone call out, "Mollie, is that you?" My heart skipped a beat when I saw Scooter standing near the front of the coffee line waving me over.

"Do you work here?" I asked.

"Up on the twenty-fifth floor." He shifted his briefcase from one hand to the other as he took a step forward to the counter. "What about you?"

I pulled a slip of paper with the details of my assignment out of my coat pocket. "I'm on the fifteenth floor."

"We're practically neighbors."

"What can I get you, sir?" the barista asked.

After Scooter ordered a large cup of the house blend, he pointed at the menu perched on top of the pastry case and asked me what I would like.

As much as I wanted to shout out, "an extra-large mocha with extra chocolate syrup," I heard my mother's voice in my head telling me to be polite and refuse the gentleman's offer at least three times. After that, then I should graciously accept, provided he wasn't an ax murderer or a punk rock band accordion player.

As I hemmed and hawed, Scooter tried again. "Cappuccino? Latte?"

Before I could politely decline again, a man behind us said, "C'mon lady. Just pick already. Some of us have jobs to get to."

Scooter smiled at me. "Tell you what. Why don't I order for you? After seeing that giant brownie sundae you had for dessert last night, I think I have an idea of what you might like." He turned to the barista. "Can you get her an extra-large mocha with extra chocolate syrup?" Then he turned back to me. "Did I get it right?"

"You did great," I said. "It's almost like you read my mind."

Scooter handed me my drink. "I don't know about mind-reading, but I feel like I know you even though we just met yesterday."

I bit my lip. "I know what you mean."

As we waited for the elevator, Scooter said, "With everything that happened last night when that waitress broke her wrist, we never got to say goodbye properly."

"Yeah, I'm sorry about that, but Eliza needed me to pitch in when she went to the hospital. Things were a bit hectic."

Scooter smiled. "I still can't get over the nicknames you gals have."

"They're not nicknames. They're roller derby names. Big difference."

"Really?" Scooter asked as we got into the elevator.

"Yes. They convey your skating personality, what you're like out on the track. Anyone can have a nickname, but not everyone can have a roller derby name. Besides, I hate nicknames. Or at least the nicknames people called me back in school. Pet names are even worse. My ex-boyfriend used to call me 'sweetie' all the time. It drove me nuts."

"I don't know. I bet I could come up with a pet name you'd like. Something original. Not any old run-of-the mill babe, hon, or sweetheart." He glanced at me. "Of course, I can't give you a pet name unless we're dating. We never did make plans for the Star Wars movie marathon."

Before we could make arrangements, the doors opened on the fifteenth floor. I scrawled down my phone number and tucked it in his coat pocket before getting out. "Call me and we'll figure something out."

"Will do," he said before holding his hand up, awkwardly pressing his index and middle finger together and his ring finger and pinky together in an attempt to make the Vulcan hand gesture popularized by Mr. Spock.

I chuckled. "That's Star Trek. But you get points for trying," I said as the doors closed.

* * *

If it hadn't been for the mocha Scooter had bought me, my morning would have been a lot worse. While my coworkers were nice, the spreadsheets I had to work with were pure agony. It was almost like who had ever set them up went out of their way to make everything as user-unfriendly as possible. And since I was the user, I was not amused.

My job was to enter data from customer satisfaction forms into various spreadsheets, then generate tables and graphs for a presentation that my supervisor was giving to senior management at the end of the week. Let me tell you, these customers were far from satisfied. You would be too if the deluxe combination salad shredder, yogurt maker, and bread machine you had purchased broke exactly one week after the warranty had expired.

Personally, I've never had the desire to make my own yogurt or bread. Isn't that what grocery stores are for? Besides, my idea of salad is the lettuce that comes on top of cheeseburgers. Still for folks who are into that sort of thing, the company television advertisements touting this appliance as the ultimate multi-tasking and space saving device sucked them right in. As I leafed through the product brochure and read about all its functionality, I began to think that I wasn't expecting enough from my espresso machine. Surely, it could also make homemade ice cream if it put its mind to it and applied itself, right?

I startled as my supervisor set another stack of

forms on my desk. Banishing thoughts of espresso flavored ice cream from my head, I set to work wrestling with spreadsheets. The only thing that made the mind-numbing data entry bearable was reading the comments customers left, like "My cinnamon oatmeal bread came out green!" and "My yogurt has chunks of dough in it!"

After totaling up satisfaction ratings and color-coding the results, it was time for lunch. Normally, I brown bagged to save money, but after the espresso fiasco, I hadn't had time to pack my usual peanut butter sandwich and Oreo cookies. There was a reasonably priced cafeteria at the hospital nearby, so I grabbed my coat and purse heading to the elevator before another stack of forms appeared on my desk.

After selecting a grilled ham and cheese sandwich with potato chips, I carried my tray to the cashier. As she rang me up, I noticed Henry sitting at a table by himself. It seemed like the perfect opportunity to find out exactly what he had been doing in the locker room yesterday.

As he crumbled crackers into his soup with one hand and leafed through a pile of papers with the other, I tapped him on the shoulder. "Mind if I sit here? It's the only open spot."

"Fancy seeing you here," he said. "I'd love to have you join me. Let me get this stuff out of the way."

After he moved a container of condiments and the papers to the side of the table, I set my tray down.

"Out on the ambulance today?" I asked.

"Yeah. Just wolfing down some food before my shift starts." After finishing his soup, he started in on his sandwich. In between bites he asked me how my arm was.

"Fine. I changed the dressing and applied more antibiotic cream like you suggested."

"No signs of infection?"

"None."

"Good. It should heal in a few days, but if you have any problems, go see your doctor. How's your other arm?"

I smiled as I pulled up my sleeve to show him. "It's fine. Doesn't need a band-aid anymore. Although I was tempted to put on that extra one you gave me, because it's so cute."

"You better save it for the next time you get an owie."

"We must keep you busy at our matches with all of our owies."

"Well, you girls do keep me on my toes. Especially you. I don't think I've ever seen anyone take as many tumbles as you do."

"Klutzy should be my middle name," I said. "Speaking of klutzy, did you hear what happened at the diner last night?" After I told him how one of the Gruesome Twosome twins had broken her arm, I cocked my head to one side. "Imagine if something like that happened during a match and there wasn't a medic to take care of it."

"That's why I'm there."

"But what if you had to leave during the match, like to go to the restroom?"

"Don't worry. I can hold it," he said with a smile.

"You know the Wild Bunch?"

"Sure. Who doesn't know them? They're legendary in the roller derby scene."

"Leon said he saw you go into the locker room during last night's game."

"He must have been mistaken." Henry fidgeted in his chair. "Why would I do that? Seriously, that would be kind of creepy sneaking in while you guys were changing."

"He said he saw you during the second half. We weren't in there then."

Henry shook his head slowly. "Wasn't me. Maybe it was someone who looked like me. Or more likely, he's mistaken. You know what he's like during the matches—laser focused on what's happening on the track. He's not paying attention to who's going into the locker room. Why are you so interested in this, anyway? Is there some sort of pervert stalking you guys?"

I thought about Leon. Sure, he was obsessed with roller derby and the players, but he wasn't really a stalker and he definitely wasn't a pervert. "No, nothing like that," I said. "I was just making conversation."

Henry raised his eyebrows. "Interesting topic of conversation—who goes in and out of the locker room." He pushed back his chair. "Well I better get going before I'm late."

As he stood and grabbed his tray, his papers fell to the ground. I bent and picked them up. "Hey, you've got spreadsheets too. Yours look a lot more interesting than mine. What is this a list of? I don't think I can pronounce anything on here." I pointed at some handwriting on one of the pages. "Oh, wait, I think I know this one. OxyContin, right? The painkiller that's so addictive."

"You better let me have that," he said as he grabbed the sheets from me. "I need to drop it off before my shift starts."

As I watched him walk away, I thought about our conversation. Henry claimed that he hadn't been in our locker room. Leon swore that he saw him though. Either Henry was lying or Leon had been mistaken. And if Leon had been mistaken, who's to say who really went into the locker room?

* * *

After lunch, I tried to concentrate on data entry, but I found myself distracted by my investigation. Misty was counting on me to find out who had taken Kyle's package so that she could get it back to him. Still all I had come up with so far was a list of suspects—Henry,

Velma, and Eliza—and now, after my conversation with Henry, that was in doubt. How was I supposed to figure out who had a motive to rob Misty's locker when I wasn't even sure who could have done it?

I glanced at the clock on my computer. It was definitely time for a break. After grabbing a coffee from the break room, I returned to my desk pulling a bag of M&M'S and a notebook from out of my purse. Opening the notebook to a blank page, I wrote down, "Skating Sleuth To Do List."

For each task I listed, I rewarded myself with a handful of the brightly colored candy. The first item on my list was to interview Leon and establish that he had really seen Henry, Eliza, and Velma go into the locker room. The next few items related to interviewing each of the suspects once they were confirmed. After tossing the empty chocolate bag in the trash can, I jotted down the final item—stock up on more M&M'S.

As the afternoon wore on, I continued to plug in numbers and type in comments, remembering to save my work frequently. If the company made such shoddy products, who knew how robust their computer systems were?

"Are you done with that batch?" My supervisor pointed at the thick stack of papers on my desk.

"Almost. Just give me a sec." I quickly typed in the last sentence from the form next to my keyboard and then placed it with the others.

She scooped them up. "The agency said you were fast," she said. "Mind working some overtime?" I considered her offer. On the one hand, some extra cash would be nice. On the other hand, spending the evening with spreadsheets didn't sound nearly as appealing as crashing on my couch watching reruns on TV. When she mentioned that the company would be providing pizza for dinner, I quickly agreed. All I had to eat at home was a jar of jalapeno peppers and the last of the Oreo cookies. Pizza sounded way better. Besides, I wasn't eager to face cleaning up the mess waiting for me in my kitchen.

By eight, I had finished the last of the data entry and even worked some magic with formulas and pivot tables. Before I headed out the door, I popped in the break room and grabbed the last piece of pepperoni for the road.

After entering the elevator, I punched the button for the ground floor. I smiled to myself remembering Scooter's lame attempt at imitating Mr. Spock. I wondered if he had tried calling me while I was stuck at the office. Not having voice mail on my landline meant I'd never know. Perhaps I would have to loiter by the coffee kiosk in the morning, hoping that he was a regular customer.

When I got out of the elevator, it was eerily quiet. The only noise was my heels clicking on the marble floor. As I made a beeline for the exit, I heard a tap-tap-tap sound behind me. I turned and saw Kyle sitting at the reception station, drumming a pen on the desk.

"Well, if it isn't Darth Skater," he said.

"What are you doing here?" I asked.

"What does it look like?" He pointed at the silver badge pinned to his crisp white shirt. "I'm the new security guard. What are you doing here?"

"I'm temping up on the fifteenth floor."

"Can you prove it?"

"How? It's not like they hand out badges that say 'Spreadsheet Specialist'."

"No, but they do give you ID tags," he said dryly.

"Oh. That's true." I handed him a boring white plastic tag. It had my name and photo on the front and a magnetic strip on the back. "A badge would be way cooler."

After examining it, he handed me a log book and pen. "You have to sign out."

While I scrawled my signature, he leaned back in his chair and yawned.

"How long are you here for?" I asked.

"All night."

"How do you stay awake?"

He pointed at a mug sitting next to the telephone. "Plenty of coffee." He stifled another yawn. "It's going to be tough getting used to the night shift after working days."

"Yeah, I heard you got laid off. Sorry about that."

He frowned. "They said it's just temporary, but I'm

not sure I actually believe them. I'm looking for something else that pays a decent wage, but so far it hasn't been easy."

"I bet it's pretty stressful," I said, passing the log book and pen back to him.

"It has been." He tapped the pen on the desk for a few moments. "Listen Mollie. I should apologize. I've been struggling to keep my temper in check and I know I've been taking it out on people like you."

"So, you mean those penalties were all bogus?"

He scowled. "No, I call them like I see them." Then his face softened. "But I don't have to be such a jerk about it ... I guess."

"It's Misty you should apologize too. She did you a favor hanging on to that jewelry. It isn't her fault it was stolen."

"I need to do my rounds," he said, pushing his chair back abruptly. "The doors are locked this time of night. Just wave your ID tag over the sensor next to the door and it will automatically open for you."

As he walked toward the bank of elevators, his phone rang. He answered it, told the other person to hang on, looked at me and then pointed at the exit.

Fine by me. Kyle was the last person I wanted to spend any more time with. As I waved my ID tag over the sensor, I remembered that I had left my to do list on my desk. If my supervisor found it before I came in, she might think I had too much time on my hands and give me an extra-large stack of satisfaction forms.

I was glad Kyle wasn't at his desk. I didn't want the hassle of having to deal with him, not to mention having to sign back in and out of the building again. Remembering how the sound of my heels echoed in the lobby, I slipped my shoes off and padded across the lobby in my socks.

While I waited for the elevator, the sound of Kyle yelling on his phone got louder and louder. Although I couldn't really make out what he was saying, I did hear him mention Misty's name. I tip-toed around the corner and saw him standing in front of the rear entrance, pacing back and forth. As he started to spin around, I ducked behind some potted plants which separated the elevator bank from that section of the lobby.

"It's that Misty girl," he said. "I left the stash with her and now it's disappeared." He paused for a moment then continued, "I don't know who took it. Maybe it was her or maybe she knows who took it. She knew what was in the package and how valuable it is. I've told her she has until Sunday to get it back or she's going to have to ..." He held the phone away from his head for a moment, then pressed it back to his ear. "Stop screaming. I heard you the first time. Don't you think I know how hard it is to get Oxycontin across the border? Remember, I'm the one who brought it across."

I startled as the elevator dinged, almost dropping my purse on the ground. Kyle whirled around and looked in my direction.

"Hang on. I heard something," he said.

I crouched down, grateful that my dark skirt and sweater helped me blend into the shadows. Kyle walked past the elevator bank, into the other side of the lobby, then back again. "It's nothing," he said. "Listen, I'll call you back. I need to finish my rounds by nine." After tucking his phone in his pocket, he opened the door to the stairwell, walked inside, and closed it firmly behind him.

I took that as my cue to leave. There was no way I was going back for my notebook now. Kyle was up to his neck in something dirty and I didn't want to spend another minute alone with him in this empty building. In my haste, I ran three full blocks before I realized that I was only in my stocking feet. As I stopped to pull on my shoes, I admitted to myself that I was going to confront Misty. The package Kyle left with her was definitely not his mother's jewelry. It was drugs. Based on how nervous she had been about going to the police about the robbery, I had a feeling that she knew exactly what it was that he had given her. What I couldn't figure out was why a sweet elementary school teacher like her was mixed up in something like that.

# CHAPTER 5
# THE ELEVATOR MOVE

"So, have you heard from Scooter? Did he call you yesterday?" Misty asked as she perched herself on a stool. We were sitting at the vintage counter in the Rock n' Roller diner sipping chocolate milkshakes. While my short legs dangled awkwardly, Misty gracefully crossed her long legs and still managed to have both her feet touch the ground.

"No. But I had to work late last night. So, if he did, I would have missed his call. And now, I'm here with you."

"You really need to get a cell phone so that people can get a hold of you when you're not at home." She looked at me slyly. "Actually, that would be the perfect excuse for you to go see him at his office. He's a telecommunications consultant. He can set you up with a phone."

"I don't want to go chasing after him," I said, conveniently leaving out that I had loitered around the coffee kiosk for a half-hour that morning hoping to run into him. "If he wants to get a hold of me, he will."

"From what Carl said, I think you can expect a call." Misty pulled a menu toward her. "I have to be at my cosmetology class in an hour, but I have time for some fries if you want to split them."

"Sure," I said. "I can always make room for fries."

"What is it you wanted to talk about, anyway?" Misty asked. "You were really mysterious on the phone last night."

I slurped down the last of my shake while I considered how to confront my friend. It's not like I could just come out and say that I thought she was involved with drugs. I needed to approach the issue more delicately and carefully consider how to manage the conversation.

"Well," Misty prompted. "You've been staring at your empty glass without saying a word."

I took a deep breath and, before I could stop myself, I blurted out, "Are you a drug dealer?" Oops, so much for tact.

Misty's eyes widened. "What?"

I put my head in my hands, took another deep breath and tried again. "I overheard someone talking last night about the package Kyle gave you. It sounded like you knew it was full of drugs."

"No, that's not true." She blew out a noisy breath. "I don't know who you heard say that, but it's just not true."

"Misty," I said, patting her hand. "It's me. You can tell me the truth."

She pulled a napkin out of the dispenser and dabbed at her eyes. "Just give me a minute."

While I waited for her to collect herself, Eliza placed a plate of fries in front of us. "Everything okay, here?" she asked when she saw Misty's expression.

"Everything's fine. She's just sad that she finished her milkshake so quickly. She's going through chocolate withdrawal," I said, giving my friend a sideways glance. She cracked a smile, then started giggling.

"Well, I can do something about that," Eliza said. "Two more shakes, coming up."

"You always know how to make me laugh," Misty said.

"You ready to talk about it?" I poured ketchup on the plate. "It'll be easier if you have some fries."

"Why don't you start," she said. "Who exactly did you overhear?"

"It was Kyle. He works as a nighttime security guard at the building I'm temping at. I overheard him on the phone telling someone that you knew that there was OxyContin in the package. It didn't sound like a personal prescription either. He said that he smuggled it across the border from Canada. So, is it true? Did you know that it was drugs?"

Misty nibbled on a few fries before answering. "Yes, I knew. But it's not what you think."

"What do I think?"

"That I'm involved in drug dealing."

"Well you are," I said, my voice raising as I thought about the trouble Misty was in. "You were in possession of illegal drugs. Drugs that were smuggled into the United States."

"Shush." Misty grabbed my arm. "Keep your voice down. Yes, I guess technically I'm involved. But it was a one-time only thing."

"That's what I don't understand. Why would you get involved? Was it because you needed the money? I know teachers don't get paid a lot, but I thought that's why you were taking that cosmetology course. That way you could make extra money working part-time doing hair and make-up."

"No, it wasn't about the money. It was about ..." Her voice trailed off as tears welled up in her eyes.

"What was it about?" I asked gently.

"It was about love."

"Love? This is about Carl?"

"Yes," she said, dabbing a napkin under her eyes. "Kyle has a compromising picture of me. He threatened to show it to Carl if I didn't do what he said."

"A picture of what? Of you and another guy?"

"Yes, but it's not what you think. It's a picture of me and Henry. It looks like we're kissing, but it's just the angle it was taken at, I swear." She paused as Eliza set two more shakes in front of us. "It happened a while ago, when Carl and I first started dating. It was after one of our matches. Henry was upset about his wife leaving him and I was comforting him. Kyle must have snapped the picture without us knowing about it."

"I don't understand. It's an innocent picture. Why don't you just tell Carl that?"

"He wouldn't understand," she said. "Kyle said that he was going to tell him that Henry and I were having an affair." She grabbed my hands and fixed her gaze on me. "I don't want to lose Carl. We have to find out who took the package, get it back to Kyle, and then we can go back to the way things should be. And we have to keep the police out of it. Promise me, please."

I was torn. Misty was my friend, a friend in a very desperate situation. Still, investigating a drug smuggling ring? It was way out of my league. I had no idea what Nancy Drew would do in a situation like this, let alone how I could really help.

My shoulders tensed as she pleaded with me. I steeled myself to say no and tell her that we should call the police. Of course, that's not what I did. Instead, I blurted out, "I promise."

* * *

After Misty left, I finished off the fries and contemplated my next move. I dug out my notebook and looked at my to do list. I had put a check mark next to "Buy more M&M'S." Yep, that one had been easy ... and delicious too. As I considered how to tackle the remaining items, I heard loud laughter behind me. I twirled my stool around and saw the Wild Bunch crowded around Leon's laptop, clearly amused by something on the screen.

I hopped down and joined them. "What's so funny, guys?"

Leon shielded the screen. "It's a surprise."

"Ooh. I love surprises," I said. "What is it?"

"If I tell you, then it wouldn't be a surprise, would it?" Leon said. "You'll have to wait until we're ready to show it to everyone."

"Hmm. When I said I like surprises, what I meant was that I love getting unexpected gifts like chocolate cupcakes and diamond earrings. What I don't like is knowing there's going to be a surprise and then having to wait for it."

"Patience is a virtue," Leon said.

"Yeah, yeah, I know. My mom always said that, especially after she pulled a tray of chocolate chip cookies out of the oven. She'd tell me to wait until they cooled down. But I'd always end up grabbing one, shoving it in my mouth, and burning my tongue."

Leon grinned. "I imagine you're the type of person who can only be patient when there are a lot of witnesses."

I smiled back. "You might be right. Now, since we've established that I'm not good with patience, can I see the surprise?"

"Go on, show her," one of the other members of the Wild Bunch said. "We could use an outsider's perspective."

"All right," Leon said. "But you have to promise something."

I groaned. The last thing I wanted was to agree to something else, especially after what I had just promised Misty. "What is it?"

"You have to promise not to tell any of the other Wild Waitresses about it."

"Oh, that's easy. I promise."

One of the guys pulled a chair over for me and I sat next to Leon. He turned the laptop toward me and hit the play button. "We've been working on a video for the team. Highlights of the matches and some bloopers."

"You're in a lot of the bloopers," the man to my left said. "Some of your falls are truly spectacular."

"Well, I guess that's one way of putting it." I rubbed my right arm. My cut was almost healed, but I still had it bandaged. I tried not to scratch at it while I watched the video. Easier said than done.

When the video was over, I congratulated them.

"Wow, that's fantastic."

"You really think so?" Leon asked.

"Absolutely. I love how you merged all the cuts together. You really captured the energy and action of roller derby."

"Did you like that one of the Gruesome Twosome squashing you between their arms when they did the elevator move?"

"I liked watching it way better than experiencing it." I touched the top of my head. "Glad I was wearing a helmet, otherwise I'd probably have a big scar here."

"Let's replay that one again," Leon said.

I leaned forward to get a closer look. If I could figure out how the twins had managed to catch me in their "elevator doors" I might be able to avoid it in the future. As the clip ended, it faded into a shot of the team skating around the track during warm-up.

"Hey, how did you take that one?" I asked. "It seems almost like an aerial view."

"I set my video camera up on the top bleacher," one of the guys said. "You can really see all the action from up there."

An idea was bubbling away in my mind, but I couldn't quite figure out what it was. As one of the waitresses skated by, I asked her for a small bowl of chocolate ice cream. Yes, I know. I had already had two chocolate milkshakes, but give me credit for showing some restraint by only asking for a small serving. Besides, I've always found that chocolate helps me think more clearly.

"It's freezing outside," Leon said. "How can you eat ice cream when it's cold enough to wear winter coats?"

"That's what scarves and mittens are for." After I ate a few spoonfuls, the fog in my brain cleared. "That's it."

"What's it?" Leon asked.

"The video of us warming-up. Was that from Sunday's match?"

"Yeah, how'd you know that?"

"Because of a certain guy in the bleachers. He's sitting right near where you usually are," I said to Leon. "See how you can partially see the hallway which leads into the locker room? You're out of the frame, but I'm positive that's the same spot."

"Okay, but how'd you know it was from Sunday?"

"Because the guy I'm talking about had never been to one of our roller derby matches until then." I felt my face grow warm as I remembered sitting in his lap. I leaned forward. "Did you have the camera sitting in that spot for the entire match?"

"We did."

"By chance do you still have the rest of the footage from that night?" When Leon nodded, I asked him to pull it up and fast forward to the second half. "We should be able to see who went into the locker room."

He crossed his arms. "I already told you who went

in there."

"Sure, but it never hurts to have corroborating evidence."

"Corroborating evidence. Are you saying you don't believe me?"

"No, it's not that," I said, quickly trying to smooth things over.

"Then what is it?"

"It's complicated, and I made a promise not to talk about it."

"Just show it to her," the guy across from me said.

As Leon advanced through the video, I wrote notes down in my notebook. Henry had walked down the hallway at the beginning of halftime, carrying his medical kit. He came back out around ten minutes later. Not long after, Velma rushed in. Eliza followed her, spending around five minutes inside, before walking back down the hall, her long coat swishing behind her. Velma was in there the longest, not leaving until close to the end of the match. She had changed into her street clothes and had a large duffel bag slung over her shoulder.

"See, that's exactly what I told you." He shut his laptop and shoved it in his backpack, rearranging a couple of books and a scarf to make it fit. As he wheeled his chair back from the table, I complimented him again on the video.

His expression softened. "Remember, you can't tell any of the other gals."

"Promise."

After the Wild Gang left, I sat back in my chair and smiled. My investigation was back on track since the suspects had been confirmed. Now I just needed to interview them. I pulled my notebook toward me and jotted down potential lines of questioning alongside a doodle I had made earlier of the Wild Waitresses logo—the skate with each of its laces in the shape of the letter W. Something was nagging me about the logo, but I was too tired to figure it out. Instead, I bundled up, wrapping my scarf tightly around me and headed home. Maybe I'd get back in time for Scooter to call.

# CHAPTER 6
# LIVE LONG AND PROSPER

By the time I got back to my apartment that night, it was after nine. Had Scooter called while I was at the diner? I stared at my phone, willing it to speak to me, but like most of the small appliances in my home, it was uncooperative and refused to answer me.

I grabbed the last two Oreo cookies, made myself a cup of hot chocolate, and headed to bed. I wanted to curl up with a cozy mystery I had checked out of the library. The sleuth in the book was a knitter and owned a craft shop. In addition to learning about what to do when you drop a stitch, I also picked up some tips on how to question suspects. The key was to bluff, making them think you already knew something and then get them to confess.

After brushing my teeth, then reading a few more

chapters, I drifted off to sleep by counting out knitting patterns in my head. The next morning, I woke up ready to do battle with the espresso machine yet again. I'm pleased to report that for this round I was victorious. Fully energized by my two mochas, I headed to the bus stop ready to whip some spreadsheets into shape.

As I walked into the office building, I peered at the coffee kiosk. No Scooter. I couldn't believe how disappointed I felt. I had only met the man twice. Sure, he had bought me a mocha and his eyes were the exact shade of my favorite dark chocolate bar. Still it was ridiculous to keep thinking about him like this, especially after what Mr. Accordion Player had put me through. I took a deep breath. If it was meant to be, it would be.

"Hold the elevator, please," a voice called out.

I quickly pressed the open button as Scooter squeezed through the doors right before they closed on him. "You just did the elevator move," I said.

"The what move?"

While I explained how the Gruesome Twosome had done their best imitation of an elevator, trapping me between their bodies during our last match, he stared at me with his puppy dog eyes.

"Lady, this is the fifteenth floor," the man next to me said. "Are you going to get out or what?"

As I reluctantly slipped out the elevator, Scooter said, "I've been trying to call you, but no one ever answers. You need a cell phone."

"I know," I said. "I don't want to miss any more calls from you." Then I gave him the Vulcan hand sign. The last thing I saw as the doors closed was the big grin on Scooter's face. Maybe this was meant to be after all.

* * *

After a day of tedious data entry, I was more than ready to let loose at practice. When I got to the warehouse, I quickly changed, stowing my belongings in my locker and making sure my padlock was securely fastened. As I exited the locker room, I noticed the door to the adjacent storage room was ajar. Although I was late to practice, I wondered what was inside. Some might call it just plain nosiness, I preferred to think of it as curiosity.

When I pushed the door open, I heard a loud crash. I turned on the light and saw a large metal box on the floor with hammers, screwdrivers, pliers, and many other assorted tools strewn around it. I gathered everything up, shoving it all into the toolbox, and placed it back on one of the large metal shelves which ran the length of the room. I looked around noticing cans of paint, sheets of plywood, and other building materials. So, this was where they stored the supplies for the warehouse renovation.

One of the paint cans was perilously perched on

the shelf. Worried that it would end up on the floor like the toolbox had, I tried to shove it further back, but it wouldn't budge. I moved it to the side and reached behind it to find the impediment. My hand felt something long and metallic. When I pulled it out, I recognized what it was immediately—bolt-cutters.

I felt a sense of satisfaction when I realized I had answered an important question in my investigation —where had the thief gotten the bolt-cutters that she or he used? It also led to another question—who knew about the contents of the storage room? I certainly hadn't until now. I was definitely going to work that into my questioning of Henry, Velma, and Eliza.

"There you are." Eliza peeked her head in the storage room. "Everyone is on the track except you. What are you doing in here anyway?"

"Oh, I was just ... um ... lost?"

"Lost?"

"I mean I was lost in a daydream. I was thinking about all the hard work that has gone into renovating the building."

"We're having another workday next weekend if you want to join us. Lots of people have volunteered. It would be great to have you there as well." She smiled. "And we're having a potluck afterward. It'll be fun."

"Are the Bruising Beauties helping out with the renovation too?"

"Sure. The Gruesome Twosome have been a big

help in particular."

"What about Velma?"

Eliza cocked her head to one side. "Yeah. She was at the last workday we had."

"So, she knows about this storage closet?"

"I guess. It's not like it's a big secret or anything." She tapped her watch impatiently. "We really need to get going. Why don't we talk about the workday and what's involved over drinks after practice?"

"That's right. You organized team drinks."

"Yep, and I invited some other folks to join us. Kyle and the other referees, the Wild Bunch, and the concession stand volunteers."

"Did you invite Henry too?"

"He said he'd be there."

"Good, I'm looking forward to seeing him," I said. What I left unsaid was that I was looking forward to questioning him about the robbery.

* * *

I have to admit that I wasn't operating at peak performance during our practice. I was distracted by the investigation and knowing that Misty was in serious trouble. Most of all what was throwing me off of my game was the fact that Scooter was sitting in the bleachers.

Carl often attended our practices, taking Misty out to dinner afterward. This was the first time anyone had come to practice to watch me. At least I assumed that's why Scooter was there. He had waved to me while holding up a gift bag. What was in the bag? Was it for me? Why hadn't he had his glasses repaired properly? How tall was he? Why was he called Scooter? Was it a nickname?

There were so many questions running through my head that I was caught off-guard when one of the girls hip checked me. When I landed on my butt as a result, Scooter rose to his feet and started to hurry over to the track. I waved him off, then made the Vulcan hand sign to let him know I was okay.

After managing to get through the rest of practice unscathed, I headed to the locker room to shower and change. While I was there, I pulled Misty aside to check on her. She said she was doing great, but the fake smile plastered on her face was less convincing than her words. I tried to fill her in on the investigation, but she seemed more interested in braiding her hair than what I had discovered about the bolt-cutters.

"Let's not think about that tonight," she said brightly. "I just want to enjoy myself over drinks, then have a nice romantic dinner with Carl. Besides, I noticed Scooter is here. You should be spending time with him instead of worrying about Kyle's silly little package."

She gathered up her stuff and walked over to chat with some of the other girls. I wondered what had happened between the previous night's state of panic and tonight where she seemed to care less about her predicament.

* * *

After practice was over, everyone gathered in the kitchen area at the back of the warehouse. The occupants of the leased office space used it during the day for lunch and coffee breaks, while we used it as a concession stand during matches. Tonight, however, Eliza was serving drinks and finger food. The room was buzzing with the sound of people's conversations and laughter bouncing off the high ceilings.

As I placed some chicken wings on a plate, I felt a tap on my shoulder that sent electric shocks straight down to my toes. "I have something for you," Scooter said holding up the gift bag.

"What is it?"

"You'll have to open it and find out."

"The bag's cute," I said, licking barbecue sauce off my fingers.

"I thought unicorns might be your thing."

"It's spooky how well you know me."

"Well, you were wearing a sweatshirt the other night with unicorns on it."

"You remembered that?"

"How could I forget? They were dressed up as ninjas." He grabbed my plate. "Why don't we find someplace to sit down."

After we positioned ourselves at the end of one of the tables, he pushed the bag toward me. "Go on."

I opened it up and pulled out a box. "Is this a phone?"

"Uh-huh."

I turned the box over in my hand. When I saw what make and model it was, I handed it back to him. "No, I can't accept this. Sorry."

"Of course, you can," he said, passing it back to me.

"No really, I can't. It's way too expensive." I locked my eyes with his. "I mean, look at you. You're still wearing those duct-taped glasses. You should spend your money on getting a new pair or getting them fixed." A wave of guilt poured over me as I placed the box on the table. "Actually, I should buy you a new pair seeing as I broke them."

Scooter smiled. "You don't need to worry about my glasses. I can afford to get them fixed. I just haven't had time yet. And the phone didn't cost me anything. Manufacturers send them to us to test. Besides, when we're done, we have to find them a good home." He inched the box toward me. "And I think you would give this one a very good home."

I tried to remember how many times I had refused Scooter's gift. Had it been two times or three? Was it okay to say yes, especially as it hadn't cost him anything? Etiquette was always so confusing. Don't even ask me what you're supposed to do with those tiny forks with two tines. Not to mention whether you're supposed to scoop your spoon outward from the bowl when you're eating soup or is that when you're eating cereal?

"Why don't I set it up for you?" Scooter offered.

"I don't know," I said.

"Tell you what how about a trade? Why don't you consider yourself to be one of our testers then? You can report any problems you have with it to me personally."

"Sounds good," I said. While Scooter worked on my new phone, Eliza came over and set two beers down in front of us. I patted the chair next to me. "You shouldn't be serving us. You aren't at work."

"It's a hard habit to break," she said. "But it would be good to get off my feet. Save me that seat and I'll be right back."

She returned with another beer and a tote bag. After taking a swig from her bottle, she pulled out a ball of turquoise yarn and knitting needles with a partially completed project on them.

"What are you making?" I asked.

"Team scarves." She held the needles up. "See how I'm working our new logo into the design on the ends." As I marveled over the intricate detail of the roller skate and laces, I realized the scarf looked familiar.

"Is this the first one you've made?"

"No. This is the second. I gave the first one to

Misty. I'm hoping to have the rest of these done by next month. I'm making one for each of you girls as a thank you for making the Wild Waitresses such a success."

"Oh, my gosh. That's so sweet of you."

As Eliza explained the pattern, which went completely over my head, Velma walked in the room. "What's she doing here?" I asked. "I thought tonight was just for our team."

"I invited her," Eliza said. "I need to speak with her about something."

"I hope it's about her attitude. Actually, I'm surprised she's still on the Bruising Beauties team after she knocked down one of the twins and broke her wrist."

Eliza looked at me sharply. "That's simply not true. Velma was feeling faint. When she grabbed the hostess stand to steady herself, she accidentally knocked into one of the twins. It was all an accident. Honestly, I don't know how these rumors get started."

While taking a sip of my beer, I contemplated all the other rumors swirling around Velma, like how she had done time in jail and in rehab. Still even if they weren't true, Velma certainly didn't do herself any favors with her tough girl demeanor. She was lucky she was such a good skater, otherwise I don't think any team would have put up with her.

Just my luck, Velma decided to sit next to me. She slouched in her chair, twirling her long red hair around her finger. Scooter looked up from the phone and pointed at the beer in front of him. "I haven't had any of it yet. Do you want it?"

"No, thanks. I'm going to stick to pop," she responded in a surprisingly polite tone before turning to Eliza. "Can we talk?"

"Sure, just give me a few minutes to finish this section and then I'll be right with you."

While Velma wandered over to the buffet table and nibbled on some crackers, I noticed the Wild Bunch in the corner. Leon had his backpack sitting on his lap and I could just make out a scarf peeking out from inside of it. It looked like a turquoise scarf with a white pattern on the end.

"I'll be back in a sec," I said to Scooter. "I need to ask Misty something."

The two lovebirds were sitting on a couch, their arms wrapped around each other, having an intimate conversation.

"Sorry, I hate to interrupt," I said. "But I need to borrow your girlfriend for a minute."

Misty shifted closer to Carl. "Have a seat."

"Actually, I was kind of hoping that we might have a word in private," I said, glancing at Carl.

"No problem. I'll give you ladies some space." He held up his empty beer bottle. "I need another one, anyway."

"Why'd you scare him off," Misty said.

"I didn't scare him off," I said. "He went to get

another beer."

"Well, what is it?"

"What's wrong with you? You're not acting like the Misty I know."

"You're overreacting," she said.

"Fine. Maybe I am, but once you hear what I have to say, you'll understand why I needed to speak with you." I pointed discretely at Leon. "I think he's the one who stole Kyle's package."

"How do you know that?"

"See that scarf hanging out of his backpack? It's the one Eliza gave you, right? The one that was missing from your locker."

"I guess so," she said skeptically.

"When he broke into your locker, he took it along with the package."

She looked dazed. "But I thought you said he wasn't a suspect."

"I really didn't think he was." I sighed. "Originally, I had believed what he told me when he said he saw Eliza, Velma, and Henry go into the locker room. Then when he showed me the video from the match—"

"What video?"

"It's what I was trying to tell you about earlier tonight. The Wild Bunch have a video showing who went into the locker room." I scratched my head. "Leon must have altered it. He cut out the part where he went into the locker room himself so that I'd suspect someone else." I took a deep breath. "We need to call the police."

Misty grew still. "No. We'll do no such thing." She chewed on her lip. "Look, I appreciate you trying to help, but I think you should stay out of it. Stop investigating. I can handle things from here."

She didn't wait for me to reply, getting up from the couch and making a beeline for Kyle. I watched as she pulled him out in to the hall. Then I put my head in my hands. What was I doing? I didn't have any business trying to investigate this robbery. Not only had I made a rookie mistake by assuming Leon wasn't a suspect, but my "client" didn't even want me on the case. I could hear my mother's voice in my head. "Stop getting mixed up in things that aren't any of your business. Your nosiness is going to get you into serious trouble one of these days."

Maybe it was time to listen to my mom's voice that lived in my head. I pushed myself off the couch, walked over to the trash can, and threw my notebook in it. My short-lived career as an amateur detective was over. I straightened my shoulders and resolved to go one step further—tomorrow I was going to look for a real job.

# CHAPTER 7
# GO BUCKEYES!

"Are you okay?" I lifted my head. Leon was leaning forward in his wheelchair and looking at me with concern. "You're sitting all by yourself looking like the world has ended."

I felt my pulse quicken as I made eye contact with him. "She knows."

"Huh?"

"Misty knows you stole the package from her locker. She's talking to Kyle now. If I were you, I'd watch yourself. He doesn't exactly seem like the forgiving type."

"What are you talking about?"

"The OxyContin. I know you took it."

"You've lost me."

"You took the scarf and the drugs. Just admit it

already." I shook my head. "You know what, never mind. I don't care what you did. It isn't any of my business."

As I started to get up from the couch, Leon wheeled closer. "You know about the scarf?" His face colored. "Please don't tell anyone I took it. I'm so embarrassed by what I did."

"I think you have a lot more to worry about than embarrassment. The police are more likely to be concerned with your possession of illegal drugs."

His brow furrowed. "Why do you keep talking about drugs?"

"The package ... it contained drugs. Drugs that you're either keeping for yourself or that you're selling." I clenched my hands in my lap. "How'd you do it anyway? How'd you doctor that video?"

"Doctor what video?" He smacked his hand on his forehead. "You mean the video I showed you at the diner last night. I didn't doctor it. I just ... well, I just edited out the last bit."

"You mean the section showing you going into the locker room."

"What do you mean? I never went in the locker room. All I did was spin around and saw that scarf lying on the floor next to the door. I recognized it as Misty's. I don't know what possessed me to take it. I just wanted something that belonged to her."

"You know that's a little creepy," I said.

"I know." He paused for a moment. "Why are you

so concerned with who went into the locker room? What is all this about drugs?"

After I explained to him what had happened, he said, "I can prove I didn't go inside." He pulled his laptop out of his backpack and turned it on. "Here's the rest of that video." I watched as Leon wheeled down the hall, stopped partway before reaching down for something out of view. When he put his hand back in his lap, it was clutching a scarf.

"How do you think it ended up there?" Leon asked. "You can't see on the video who dropped it."

"Maybe it got caught up on Henry's medical kit and then fell off in the hall? I'm not really sure. It seems like there's a lot of guesswork when it comes to investigations." I rubbed my eyes. "So, if you didn't take the drugs, then it's back to being Henry, Velma, or Eliza."

"Misty really should call the police."

"Don't you think I know that? I'm tempted to call them myself." I looked up as I saw Kyle and Misty come back into the room. "Except I can't since I promised."

"Tell you what," Leon said. "Why don't I help you with the investigation?"

"I think you've got bigger things to worry about," I said as Kyle walked toward us. "I think you better show him that video before he beats the crap out of you."

* * *

After we managed to convince Kyle that Leon hadn't taken the drugs, Leon took off in a hurry.

Then Kyle surprised me by asking me to continue the investigation. "Misty told me that you're pretty good with this stuff."

I raised my eyebrows. "She did?" Misty stared at the floor, refusing to meet my eyes.

"Yeah." He drummed his fingers on the coffee table in front of the couch. "I've got to go out of town for a few days. I don't have time to deal with this. So, you're going to do it for me."

"Me?"

"Yep. I'm meeting my ... um, contact on Sunday. You have until then to get the package to me."

"But why me? I'm not involved in this."

Kyle smirked. "Really? You're involved up to your eyeballs. I told you to stay out of my business, but you stuck your nose in it anyway. So, you're going to finish what you started. Find out who stole the Oxy and get it back or else ..." He gave Misty a meaningful look.

"Or what, you're going to show that picture to Carl? That's your threat? Carl will see right through your scam."

Kyle pulled a switchblade out of his pocket and coolly tossed it back and forth between his hands. "I think we've moved way beyond a photo, don't you?"

He put the knife back in his pocket and then patted me on my back. "I think we understand each other, don't we?"

I stared in disbelief as he walked over to the fridge. He pulled out a beer, then joined Carl and Scooter in the corner, chatting away as though he didn't have a care in the world.

"I'm sorry," Misty said, her voice cracking. "I'm sorry for everything ... getting you involved in the first place, then for shutting you out, and now for this."

I took a deep breath. "Don't worry. We'll figure it out."

"But how? It's Wednesday and we only have until Sunday to find out who did it."

* * *

By the time Saturday rolled around, I was in a complete state of panic. The only thing I had managed to accomplish since Wednesday was to enter data into spreadsheets. My supervisor kept piling stacks of customer satisfaction forms on my desk. While the overtime pay was great, I hadn't found an opportunity to track down my suspects—Henry, Velma, and Eliza—and continue my investigation. To be honest, even if I had found time to question them, I had no idea what I would have asked them.

What kept me going were the texts that Scooter

sent me on my new phone. He must have found some sort of sci-fi trivia site. Since I was pretty sure he couldn't have come up with things like, "Never tell me the odds," and "Live long and prosper," by himself.

After tossing and turning most of Friday night, I really needed an extra-large, extra-chocolaty mocha the next morning. My espresso machine decided to have a temper tantrum—spitting out clouds of dark smoke and making a loud screeching noise—causing me to have to stop at my neighborhood coffee shop before I was due at the warehouse.

The two teams were meeting up at nine, then riding a chartered bus to Columbus for our exhibition match. While I wasn't thrilled about the long drive, at least it would give me a chance to corner Eliza and Velma. Maybe I could find out more about their movements last Sunday.

After we boarded the bus, Eliza said, "In honor of our match in Columbus, home of the Ohio State Buckeyes, I made buckeyes for the trip," Everyone cheered as she walked down the aisle passing out the candy.

"What is it?" one of the Bruising Beauties asked.

"I forgot you're a recent transplant to Ohio," Eliza said. "You mix together peanut butter, powdered sugar, butter, and vanilla, roll the mixture into balls, chill them, and then you dip them in chocolate to finish them."

"You have to leave a small portion of peanut butter showing at the top though so it resembles the nut from our state tree, the buckeye," Misty said. "They're delicious."

The Bruising Beauty took a bite and sighed contentedly.

When Eliza neared the back of the bus, I patted the seat next to me. "I saved a spot for you."

As she sank back into the upholstery, she handed me the candy box. It contained one lone buckeye. I heard my mother's voice telling me it would be rude to take the last one. She was probably right too, but I couldn't help myself, shoving it in my mouth before Eliza changed her mind.

"Excited for the match?" she asked.

"I am." I stretched my arms out in front of me and yawned. "But I wish I had slept better last night."

"I know what you mean," she said. "I had a hard time falling asleep."

"Why's that?"

"Did you ever wonder how you're going to pay the bills?"

"Constantly. But I'm a temp living in a crummy rented apartment and I ride the bus." I ticked items off with my fingers. "You have that nice house in Shaker Heights. You own the diner. You own the warehouse. You lease out space in the warehouse, and you–"

Eliza stopped me by covering my hand.

"Appearances can be deceiving. It's really the bank that owns everything." She shook her head. "I shouldn't be burdening you with my worries."

"That's what friends are for." I looked across the aisle where Misty was sitting staring blankly out the window. "We help each other out."

"You're right about that." She pulled her knitting out of her bag. As she positioned her needles she said, "I don't know why I'm so worried. I think I've figured out a solution to my cash flow problems, but I can't relax until I'm sure everything's in place though."

As Eliza worked away at the turquoise scarf, I felt sick. Not only had Eliza had an opportunity to steal the package, she also had a motive. Those drugs were worth a pretty penny. A pretty penny that might keep the bank off her back.

***

I didn't have a chance to speak with Velma until halftime. Although she rode on the bus with us, she was sitting on the sidelines, not playing for the Bruising Beauties.

"Still sick?" I asked.

Velma rubbed her stomach and grimaced. "Yeah. Must be something I ate."

"Why didn't you stay home and rest?"

"I wanted to be here to support the team."

"When do you think you'll be back at it?"

"I'm not sure. It could be a while."

I furrowed my brow. "If your stomach bug isn't going away, don't you think you should see a doctor?"

"Oh, uh, it isn't just that. I also did something to my back. The pain is unbearable."

I thought back to the rumors about Velma being in rehab for pain pills. Maybe she had stolen the drugs for her own personal use.

"Do you take anything for it like OxyContin?"

Her eyes widened. "Are you kidding? Do you know how dangerous that stuff is? I had a cousin who was addicted to that stuff." She touched her belly and smiled. "Besides, I don't think Oxy would be good for my stomach problem."

"What's this about you being sick?" a voice asked from right behind us.

I turned and saw Henry holding his medical kit. "I didn't hear you sneak up on us."

"Soft soles," he said, pointing at his sneakers. "They don't make any sound. I actually came over to tell you that Eliza is looking for the two of you. Something about a group picture of the two teams."

"Okay," I said, getting to my feet.

As I picked up my helmet from the bench, Henry grabbed it from me. "I'll hang on to this for you. You don't want to be wearing that in the photo."

"Thanks," I said. "You coming, Velma?"

"I think I'll stay here," she said. "Eliza will understand."

* * *

Things were going great during the second half. The Wild Waitresses were ahead and the crowd was cheering. I had just executed a fantastic "truck and trailer" move with Misty acting as the truck and me hanging on to her while she pulled me through the pack.

Then I felt someone slam into me and everything went dark.

"Mollie, Mollie ... are you okay?"

I opened my eyes and saw Misty kneeling over me. "What happened?"

"You had a really bad fall," she said. "No, hang on, don't try to get up. Let Henry check you first."

After a few minutes of Henry assessing me for injuries, I propped myself up against the bench. I rubbed the back of my neck, then pulled it away when I felt something sticky. "Is that blood?" I asked as I looked at my hand.

"Did she say blood?" I looked up. Scooter was standing a few feet away, looking like he was going to pass out.

As Henry pressed a bandage to the back of my head, I said. "You should probably take care of him instead. I think I can handle the blood better than he can."

"Hey, fellow, sit down on the bench," Henry said. "I don't need two patients to deal with." Then he turned to me. “The ambulance is on its way.”

“Ambulance? Why? It’s just a cut. Head wounds always bleed a lot, even when they’re minor.”

“True, but you could have a concussion.”

“How did I end up cutting my head, anyway?”

Misty held up my helmet. “It looks like your strap broke and it came off your head when you fell. You’re lucky you weren’t more seriously injured.”

While Henry walked over to meet the EMTs, Scooter inched over on the bench. “Are you sure you’re okay?”

“Other than a headache, I feel fine. Nothing a band-aid can’t cure.” I reached into the pocket of my waitress outfit. Since I hadn’t had time to get it washed since our previous match, I knew the kids band-aid would still be in there. “See, one of these will fix me right up.” Then I looked at what I was holding in confusion. There was not just one, but two band-aids in my hand.

As I watched Henry help the EMTs wheel the stretcher over, I felt my blood go cold. “It was Henry,” I said in a whisper.

“What did you say?” Misty asked, leaning down to hear me.

“Henry stole the OxyContin and I think he tried to kill me.”

# CHAPTER 8
# AN AWFUL WASTE OF SPACE

After spending a few hours in the ER, I was finally given the all clear. The team had already gone back home on the bus, but Misty waited at the hospital with me. It turns out she wasn't the only one. When the nurse wheeled me out into the lobby, Scooter was standing there holding a bouquet.

"How are you feeling?" he asked as he handed the flowers to me.

"Fine." I pointed at the back of my head. "Just a few stitches. The doctor said all the tests for a concussion came back negative."

"Carl's pulling the car up front," Misty said. "We should have you home by seven."

When we got to the outskirts of Cleveland, I convinced them to stop by the diner before dropping me off. Eliza had sent me a text on my new cell phone asking how I was doing and letting me know that she had a present for me.

When we walked through the doors, the Gruesome Twosome gave me a giant bear hug, telling me that they were glad I was okay. If they had been actual bears, I don't think they could have hugged me any harder.

"Hey, watch her head," Misty said.

"Are you sure you don't want to go home?" Scooter asked.

"Not without a chocolate milkshake," I said with a grin.

Eliza skated past. "Did I hear something about needing a milkshake? Grab a table and I'll bring one over right away." Not only did Eliza bring me a shake, she also brought a giant plate of fries. As I dug in, she pulled a chair up next to me.

"What happened after we went with Mollie to the hospital?" Misty asked Eliza.

"The police came and arrested Henry," she said. "They also have an APB out on Kyle, but they think he's already fled the country to Canada."

Misty fidgeted nervously with the salt and pepper shakers. Carl took them away from her. "It's okay, babe," he said stroking her hair soothingly.

"How did you know it was Henry who was responsible?" Eliza asked.

"It all came down to a band-aid."

"A band-aid?" Eliza asked incredulously. "You identified a drug dealer based on a band-aid?"

"I know. It's crazy, right? Who knew medical supplies would be the key to the whole case?" I explained about the kids band-aids that Henry had kept in his medical kit. "There were two green ones. Some had cats on them and others even had dinosaurs. He put a kitty-cat one on my arm and gave me an extra one just like it. I tucked it in the pocket of my skating outfit and didn't think about it again. When Misty's locker was broken into and we were going through her stuff, one of the kids band-aids fell onto the floor. I assumed it had fallen out of my pocket at the time and tucked it back in there. Then when I had my accident today and Scooter came over to check on me, he was a little freaked out by the blood."

"I wasn't freaking out," Scooter said.

Carl slapped his shoulder. "Of course you were, man. You can barely deal with blood from a paper cut."

"Just go on with your story," Scooter said.

"So, I tried to lighten the mood by pulling the kids band-aid out of my pocket. Except there wasn't just one band-aid in there. Nope, instead there were two. One with cats and one with dinosaurs."

"And Henry had only given you one extra band-aid," Eliza said.

"Correct. That meant the one we found on the

locker room floor had to be one that he dropped. It must have fallen out when he was hiding the OxyContin in his medical kit. He had been on my suspect list, but I hadn't had a chance to question him properly."

"Girl, you sound like a regular Nancy Drew," Eliza said. "Who else did you suspect?"

"Uh, no one really."

"She suspected you and Velma," Misty blurted out. When she saw the look on Eliza's face, her face reddened. "Sorry. It's just that you were on the video tape."

Eliza crossed her arms. "Care to explain?"

"We knew that Misty's locker was broken into during the second half of the match that day. The Wild Bunch had a video of who went in and out of the locker room during that time. There were only three people on it—you, Velma, and Henry."

"Okay, that's true. Velma and I were in there. But why would you suspect us?"

"The two of you both knew that there were bolt-cutters in the storage closet next to the locker room so you would have been able to easily grab them and break the padlock open."

"Henry knew about them too," Eliza said. "He borrowed them a few weeks ago to cut a bike chain off."

"Ah, I was wondering about that," I said.

Eliza pursed her lips. "But just knowing about the

bolt-cutters shouldn't have made us suspects. What motive could we possibly have had?"

"Well, you told me that you're having financial troubles and Velma has a history of drug problems," I said trying to choose my words carefully.

"Do you really think that I would stoop so low as to use drug dealing to solve my money problems? And all those rumors about Velma are just that, rumors plain and simple. She's never touched a drug in her life. Sure, she likes to pretend that she's a tough girl, have this whole mean skater persona, but she's actually insecure deep down."

"Why did you go to the locker room?" I asked.

"Velma asked me to meet her there. She hasn't been feeling well lately and she was worried that she's ... you know what, never mind about Velma. Tell me more about Henry."

"Oh, my gosh," I said, putting the puzzle pieces together. The other night, Velma had drunk root beer, rather than a beer, she had felt faint at the diner, and now she had "stomach" problems. "She's pregnant, isn't she? That's why she's been sick and it explains why she didn't skate today."

"Shush," Eliza said. "It's early days. Let her tell you in her own time. Now, back to Henry. Why did he do it?"

"I'm not sure, but I think he had two motives, really. He was struggling to make ends meet being a single dad, so it could have been for the money. But he also hated Kyle for stealing his ex-wife away. Maybe he took the drugs so that Kyle would be in trouble with whoever is heading up the drug smuggling ring."

"Revenge is a powerful motive," Carl said. "But, don't worry. No matter why he did it, Henry is going to serve time and so will Kyle once they track him down." He squeezed Misty's hand. "Those guys deserve punishment for what they did to you, babe."

Misty's eyes welled up as she squeezed his hand back. Then she turned to me. "I'm so sorry I got you mixed up in all this."

"It's okay. That's what friends are for."

"But Henry tried to kill you." Misty looked at Eliza. "We looked at Mollie's helmet on the drive back up here. We think he partially cut through the strap, hoping the rest of it would break the next time she fell."

"When did he have a chance to do that?" Eliza asked.

"Remember when you sent him over to tell me about the group photo? Well, he offered to hold my helmet for me. While everyone was distracted, I think he used one of the scalpels in his medical kit to make the cut."

"Mollie thinks that he overheard her talking with Velma about OxyContin." Misty said. "He probably figured that I had already told her about what was stolen from my locker. He was afraid that she might find out what had really happened and wanted to stop her before she did."

"He's really sneaky," I said. "I didn't even hear him behind Velma and me until he actually said something."

"I think he did the same thing to Kyle and me. He must have overheard Kyle ask me to hold the package of Oxycontin for him," Misty added.

"After everything you've been through and what you've done for Misty, you deserve something for yourself." Eliza pulled a tissue-wrapped parcel out of her tote bag and placed it in front of me.

"Ooh. I think I know what this is." I tore the paper off and squealed in delight. "I was right. One of your beautiful team scarves." I gave Eliza a kiss on the cheek, before wrapping it around my neck. "Thanks for everything. The team wouldn't be the same without you." Then I lowered my voice. "And I hope your money problems work themselves out soon, too."

"They already have. In fact, I need to go meet my new investors now," she said, pointing at the Gruesome Twosome.

"Them, really?"

"Didn't you know? They made a killing developing some customer satisfaction software. It's used by a lot of companies, including one based here in Cleveland. You know the one with the ads on TV for those combination bread, yogurt, salad shredding appliances? Now they want to reinvest their proceeds into the diner. The only reason they've been waitressing here was to check out the operation before approaching me with an offer."

My jaw dropped as I watched Eliza chat with the twins. They were the ones who had designed the spreadsheet software I used at my temp job?

"We're going to have to catch you guys later," Carl said to Scooter and me. He wrapped his arm around Misty's shoulders. "You ready, babe?"

She took a deep breath. "I'm ready."

As they walked out the door, Scooter explained that Carl was going to the police station with her. "He's talked to the D.A. about her case. Considering the threats Kyle made on her life and the fact that she's cooperating fully, they should go easy on her."

"So, he's going to stand by her through this? He comes from a family of police officers. How do they feel about him dating someone who was caught up in smuggling Oxycontin?"

"He told me that he doesn't really care what anyone thinks. He loves her. It's as simple as that."

* * *

After we left the diner, Scooter convinced me to drive to the lake and go for a walk along the waterfront.

As we got out of the car, I said, "Wait, it's freezing out here."

"But you have your nice new scarf to keep you warm," he said as he tucked it more securely around my neck. "It's a beautiful night out. Let's go see if we can spot a falling star and make a wish."

"What are you going to wish for?"

He gazed at me with those dark brown eyes of his. "You know, I think my wish has already come true." Then he grabbed my hand and led me down to the docks.

I pointed at a sleek looking powerboat. "Carl talked to his police friends. They think that's how Kyle got the drugs in from Canada. He would take his buddy's boat out to the international boundary where a guy from Ontario would hand the Oxycontin off to him."

"It looks like a fast boat," Scooter said. "But there's something to be said for taking things slowly. See that sailboat over there?" I nodded. "Wouldn't it be great to buy one of those and sail off into the sunset?"

I shivered as the wind picked up. "Sounds cold to me."

"Well, obviously Lake Erie in the fall isn't ideal." He stared off at the horizon. "But sailing in the Caribbean, now that would be something."

"Is that your dream? Owning a sailboat and running off to some deserted island?"

He laughed. "No, I'm just being silly. I've got a great job and good friends in Cleveland. Besides, now I've met you. Why would I want to leave?"

"You're lucky that you like what you do," I said.

"Temping isn't exactly glamorous."

"Well, if you could do anything, what would you do?"

I looked down at the dock. "Oh, I don't know."

Scooter lifted my chin. "I think you do know. You can tell me. If you could do anything in the world, what would it be?"

"You promise not to laugh?"

"I promise."

"Pinky promise?"

"I'll do you one better than that." He held up his hand and extended his fingers in a now familiar move. "I'll Vulcan promise you."

"You know what Vulcans are?"

"I'll have you know that I watched an episode of *Star Trek* last night. It was kind of strange. All these small furry creatures reproducing like crazy."

"Tribbles. They're called tribbles," I said after a loud fit of giggles. "Aren't they adorable?"

"They're cute," he admitted. "But I'd never want one as a pet. I'd get a cat before I ever got one of those things. Now, you've managed to avoid the subject of our discussion. What would be your dream career?"

"I want to investigate UFO sightings and alien abductions." I paused to gauge Scooter's reaction. "You're not laughing."

"Why would I laugh?"

"Most people laugh when I tell them. Or, in my mother's case, have a fainting spell."

"You don't have to worry about me laughing. Why would I laugh at someone's dreams? And I don't think you have to worry about me fainting." Scooter gently touched the back of my head. "As long as you don't start bleeding again, that is. Does it still hurt?"

"I can't feel a thing. But then again, I can't feel my toes either, because it's freezing out here."

"Let's head back," Scooter said.

As he turned to walk back to the car, I grabbed his hand. "Did you see that? It was a falling star." As we gazed into the sky, I said, "The universe is a big place. There has to be life out there somewhere."

Scooter looked up into the sky. "Well, if there wasn't, it'd be an awful waste of space."

"That line's from my favorite movie of all time."

"What movie?"

"*Contact*. It's a book by Carl Sagan that was made into a movie. You just quoted a line from it. It's about a scientist who works on the SETI program trying to find evidence of alien life to prove that we're not alone. It stars—"

Scooter cupped my face with his hand. "Shush. I don't know anything about *Contact* or SETI or alien life. All I know is that, right now, it feels like we're the only two people in the whole universe." Then he pulled me toward him and kissed me. In that moment, as his lips pressed against mine, I knew he was the only person in the universe for me.

# AUTHOR'S NOTE

Thank you so much for reading *Robbery at the Roller Derby*! If you enjoyed it, I'd be grateful if you would consider leaving a short review on Goodreads and/or your favorite retailer. Reviews help other readers find my books and encourage me to keep writing.

My experiences buying our first sailboat with my husband in New Zealand (followed by our second sailboat in the States), learning how to sail, and living aboard our boats inspired me to write the *Mollie McGhie Sailing Mysteries*. You could say that there's a little bit of Mollie in me.

Having grown up in Cleveland, Ohio, I had a lot of fun writing this prequel and including references to my home state, such as buckeyes. Is there anything better than chocolate and peanut butter candy?

Want to find out what happens next for Mollie? Check out *Murder at the Marina*. Spoiler alert: Mollie and Scooter got married, moved to Florida, and are celebrating their tenth wedding anniversary. When Scooter gives Mollie a dilapidated sailboat as an anniversary gift, she's not impressed. When a dead body turns up on board, things get even worse.

# ABOUT THE AUTHOR

Ellen Jacobson is a chocolate obsessed cat lover who writes cozy mysteries and romantic comedies. After working in Scotland and New Zealand for several years, she returned to the States, lived aboard a sailboat, traveled around in a tiny camper, and is now settled in a small town in northern Oregon with her husband and an imaginary cat named Simon.

Find out more at ellenjacobsonauthor.com

# ALSO BY ELLEN JACOBSON

**Mollie McGhie Cozy Sailing Mysteries**

Robbery at the Roller Derby
Murder at the Marina
Bodies in the Boatyard
Poisoned by the Pier
Buried by the Beach
Dead in the Dinghy
Shooting by the Sea
Overboard on the Ocean
Murder aboard the Mistletoe

**Smitten with Travel Romantic Comedies**

Smitten with Ravioli
Smitten with Croissants
Smitten with Strudel
Smitten with Candy Canes
Smitten with Baklava

**North Dakota Library Mysteries**

Planning for Murder